Ruth Gogoll's
Christmas Carol

I0548892

Ruth Gogoll's

Christmas Carol

Translated from the German by
Susanne M. Swolinski

© 2010
édition el!es
www.elles-books.com

Translation by Susanne M. Swolinski
Edited by Shari J. Berman

Cover Photo shows the Christmas market in Annaberg-Buchholz, Germany
© Pixstore – Fotolia.com
ISBN 978-3-941598-07-2

eave me alone. I don't want anything to do with bloody Christmas!" Just the thought of the upcoming holiday got Michaela's blood boiling.

"Ms. Wittling, you can't ignore it any longer, we have to talk about it now." Her secretary, a calm and composed woman in her mid-fifties, was unwavering. Those many years working for the Wittlings had taught her perseverance. "Your employees are entitled to a few days off. Have you thought about the holiday bonus yet?" She raised a questioning eyebrow.

"What? Days off? A bonus?" Michaela asked, getting more and more agitated. "They are off all the time anyway; that alone costs a fortune! Now you want me to give them a bonus? For what? A Christmas bonus so they can go and spend money on gifts? Go shopping in their free time while I'm working? Nobody is giving me any gifts, why should I give them?"

"We're not talking about gifts," her secretary reminded her patiently. "Your employees are legally entitled to it all."

Michaela Wittling, Mike to some and only on special

occasions, rose to her imposing six feet two inches. Her dark hair fell into her face and made her look even more menacing. "Bad enough," she said, "that the government is supporting this kind of extravagance and idleness."

"May I ...?" A blond woman of slight build stepped over the threshold of Michaela's office and stopped.

"What?" Michaela barked at her as if this one employee was responsible for the misery she was facing at that moment.

"I'm sorry, I ... please forgive me; I did not mean to interrupt." The young woman began to withdraw.

"Come on, spit it out already." Michaela drummed her fingers impatiently on the desk. "I can't stand this kind of submissive behavior. Just tell me what you want!"

"I ... I heard that the company won't be closing over the holidays, that we are allowed to come and work. I thought ... well, I mean ... if it's possible ... I would like to take the opportunity and catch up on a few things and finish them before the end of the fiscal year."

Michaela was stunned for a moment. Surprised, she raised her eyebrows, but quickly drew them together again. "Because of the double time, right? You let the work add up until it's too late, and then you'll be getting paid double because you're working on a holiday."

"No ..." The young woman slowly raised a hand as if to ward off a bad spirit. "No, that's not how it is. I just noticed last year ... it's simply not feasible to get the work done before the holidays. There are always so many orders coming in at that time. The balancing of the books gets delayed. That leads to trouble with the Tax Office. Then we'll have to pay fines, which we could avoid if I work over the holidays. That way I could submit the annual balance sheets on time. I ... I don't even want to be paid any double time." Her eyes had been searching the floor while she had spoken. Now she lifted them and looked up at Michaela, as if she were asking for approval of an outrageously audacious suggestion. "I just want everything to be correct and on time."

"You are entitled to double time, Ramona; you can't waive it," Michaela's secretary commented. "And I, for one, like your idea. We would save much more than we'd have to pay you extra," she said with a sly sideways glance at Michaela.

Michaela sat down, still drumming her fingers on the desk, though much less impatiently and intensely as before. "Is that correct?" She looked at her secretary. "We would save something?"

"That's right," her secretary confirmed, nodding her head. "But, don't you need to be with your daughter?" she asked Ramona. "Will she not miss her mother on Christmas Eve? She's still quite small, isn't she?"

"She –" Ramona started to sway. "She will have to be in the hospital over Christmas."

"Over Christmas?" The secretary's voice sounded appalled.

"There's no other way, she – it's a difficult treatment." Ramona looked at the floor again. She was shaking so hard by now, she was wishing for a chair.

"All right," Michaela said. She did not seem to have listened to that last exchange. "You'll be working over Christmas. I will be here, too, as always." She dismissed Ramona with an impatient wave of her hand.

❧ ❦ ❧ ❦

"Mommy, mommy, mommy!" The little girl rushed towards her mother as if she had not seen her for at least a year.

"Sweetheart." Ramona knelt down, dropped her handbag, and embraced her daughter. "My sweetheart," she repeated and hid the tears that threatened to fall in the hair of the little girl she now hugged close.

"I told her not to run so fast, but as soon as she saw you, nothing could hold her back." The pediatric nurse stopped next to them and smiled.

"But, does she have to –" Ramona gathered her daughter in her arms and stood up with her. Leonie was already five years old, but so small and slender that Ramona did not have any problems lifting her. She looked more like three. "Does she have to take it slowly?" Ramona's voice sounded scared. She looked at the nurse with trepidation.

"Oh, no, not at all." The nurse laughed. "She's doing fine, our little pumpkin." She playfully pinched the little one's cheek. The girl made a face and tried to wriggle away from the hand.

Ramona let her daughter down. At the end of the long hospital corridor, she could see a little boy waving to them.

"Mommy, come with me. Let's go play with Florian," Ramona's daughter demanded, pulling on her hand.

"Just a minute, Leonie." Ramona gave her daughter a loving smile. "I have to talk to Nurse Johanna; then I'll be there. You go ahead."

"Promise, Mommy," Leonie replied forcefully. "Or

else I won't go."

"I promise." Ramona patted her head. "Don't worry. Go ahead, and I'll be right there."

Leonie gave her a skeptical look, but as soon as she remembered Florian at the other end of the corridor, she forgot everything else and ran towards him.

Ramona looked on while Leonie's figure seemed to shrink more and more, until she finally disappeared into the playroom with Florian. "She seems to be doing fine," she remarked, trying to sound hopeful. "If you say so, too —"

"I only said that because the child was present," was Nurse Johanna's grave reply. She looked at Ramona with sadness in her eyes. "Today's test results were not promising. Her cheerfulness is deceiving. She's fooling us all by always being in such a good mood. She lifts everybody up with her cheery disposition."

"She has spent half her life here." Ramona's voice hinted at the bitterness she felt. "You know her better than I do."

"You have to be strong." The nurse touched her shoulder. "You know that with a congenital defect like hers most children die within the first few months. Leonie has survived a long time."

"Because she's five?" Ramona started to falter, and the nurse led her to a chair. "Five years old? Is that supposed to be all? Is that a whole life?"

"We can't change that, as terrible as it is." The nurse's hand returned to Ramona's shoulder and gave her a comforting squeeze. "We can't change it and neither can you. We did everything we could."

"Everything you could do for somebody with public health insurance, you mean," Ramona replied bitterly.

She looked at the nurse. "I'm sorry. None of it is your fault."

"No, it isn't." The nurse gave her a sympathetic smile. "And it's not the doctors' fault, either. Even without the reforms to our health system, we wouldn't be able to do anything. We have exhausted all options. There are no other recognized therapies in Germany, or anywhere else in Europe."

"Only in America," Ramona said softly.

"There is no guaranteed success," the nurse objected. "That's why insurance won't pay for it."

"How can that be?" Ramona asked with a weak voice. "Old people who want to die, who have lived their lives and experience permanent pain, are being forced to live, to suffer – but my daughter, who still has her whole life ahead of her . . . is being sentenced to death, just because there is not enough money."

"I know you're desperate. It seems so utterly unjust." All the compassion she felt for Ramona and Leonie was clearly evident in the nurse's voice. "Many of those people would give everything to be finally allowed to die, and maybe that would free up the money for other treatments. No –" She interrupted herself. "We can't talk like this. We shouldn't even be thinking it."

"No, you're right. We shouldn't." Ramona squared her shoulders and wiped away the tears that had been streaming down her cheeks. "It would be inhumane. We can't offset one life with another. Maybe there is a higher power that knows what it's doing. I always hope . . ." She swallowed. "I always hope that all of it makes sense somehow, even if I can't perceive it."

"It is comforting to believe in something." The nurse nodded in approval. "Be glad you still can. Many parents lose their faith in situations like these."

"I can understand that. Still, I don't think my daughter should suffer just because I wanted her to be born." Ramona said with determination and pushed herself off the chair.

"Don't." The nurse grabbed Ramona's arms and tried to look into her eyes. "Don't blame yourself. That only makes things worse. You did nothing wrong. All the tests during your pregnancy were fine. Nobody could have anticipated anything."

"Maybe I'm being punished," Ramona said. "Maybe I should have been a better person."

"Ms. Benckhoff! Stop it right there!" The nurse shook her lightly. Trying to talk some sense into her, she said, "You are the most decent person I know, the most loving mother. You work yourself to death for your daughter and spend every free moment with her. There's nothing more you can do. You have to accept it. You can't keep blaming yourself."

"That's easier said than done." Ramona's sigh betrayed her exhaustion. "If Leonie had a father, maybe he would have the money to —"

"Every child has a father," the nurse interrupted with a confused look on her face.

"Biologically, yes." Ramona shook her head. "But that's of no use in this case." She turned away from the nurse and walked down the corridor. When she reached the playroom, she squared her sagged shoulders again and put on a smile that almost seemed genuine. "Hey, you little troublemakers!" She entered the room. "Whatcha doin'?"

❦❦❦❦

Mike? Is that you?"

Michaela had just entered her apartment and now stopped for a moment, before continuing on to the living room, from where she had heard the voice. "What are you doing here?" she snapped at the woman sitting on her couch.

Karina held up a key. It jingled slightly. "You gave this to me. Did you forget?" A small smile crept over her face.

"Yes, I did indeed forget." Michaela set down her briefcase and placed her own keys on the table. "Are you here to give it back to me?"

"Well ..." Karina got up and walked over to Michaela, a smile playing at her lips. "Well, I had hoped I could keep it a while longer."

"As a reward for entering my apartment while I'm not home, without my consent, and without informing me?" Michaela raised an eyebrow.

"Do I have to?" Karina smiled seductively. "I thought I would surprise you. Don't you like that?"

"I hate surprises," Michaela growled. She took the key from Karina's fingers and put it into her pocket.

"But, Mike ... Micky ... my lady love ..." Karina purred. She came closer to Michaela until their bodies touched. Michaela did not move. Karina's hand slowly moved between Michaela's thighs and came to a rest on her crotch. "You like this, don't you?" Her hand pressed against Michaela's pubic bone, gently at first, then more forcefully. "Come on," she whispered. "Let go. Don't always be so grim."

Michaela felt the tingling Karina's hand caused. But she disapproved, because she was mentally unprepared for the encounter. She had been expecting an empty apartment – and now this. No. She really did not appreciate surprises. She turned away. "I think you'd better go now," she remarked gruffly. "I still have work to do."

"Work! It's all you ever do." Karina sounded annoyed. "Don't you ever have time for a private life?"

"I don't need a private life. My work satisfies me completely." Michaela edged further away from Karina.

Karina moved gracefully through the room and snuggled against Michaela's back. "Well, that's not completely true." She snickered quietly. "Or else we'd never have met." This time her hand moved between Michaela's legs from behind.

Michaela flinched. "I told you the first time that it would also be the last time. I don't have time for more."

"Yes, you said that," Karina drawled. "But we've met again since then."

"Because you keep coming back." Michaela spun around. Karina's hand lost its position between her legs. Michaela felt relieved, because the tingling had become more intense. "I stick to random encounters, because that's the most sincere form of interaction. I don't want to raise any hopes I can't fulfill. One night – that's simple and clear. I don't need more, and I don't want more. My business gets the highest priority."

"Oh, really," Karina sneered. "Of course, it does. It's all you ever do. It's hard to believe your sexual needs ever put in an appearance at all." The corners of her mouth twitched with irony.

"That kind of need . . ." Michaela inhaled deeply. "It has a much lower priority. But that's beyond your grasp."

"No, I don't understand that. You got that right." Karina still looked at her with an ironic glint in her eyes. "You satisfy 'those kinds of needs,' as you call them so infrequently, I'm surprised you haven't imploded yet."

"Maybe I will one day." Michaela replied with a steady voice. "But that is none of your concern."

"And if I were to make it my concern?" Karina's smile became seductive again. "If I made it my concern to keep that from happening?" She moved closer to Michaela, stopped only inches away from her and looked up into her eyes.

"Aren't there enough other women out there who want to have sex with you?" Michaela sounded extremely harsh.

"They aren't you." Karina's voice had again taken on a quite distinctive purr. "You are unique, my lady love." She leaned forward and rested her head against Michaela's breast.

Michaela did not move and thought about kicking Karina out, but at the same time she felt the desire Karina's advances had initiated. It really had been some time. "You're like a barnacle," she said. "Every attempt to get rid of you is a waste of time. And if there's something I hate more than surprises, then it's inefficiency."

She bent down and kissed Karina forcefully.

❧⦿❧

The next morning, Karina was gone. She knew Michaela could be unpleasant if she did not wake up alone in her bed. That was something Karina decided to respect.

Michaela had no need for an alarm clock to wake up. She opened her eyes at exactly the same time, 5:30 a.m., every day, every week, every year. Since she had taken over running the family business, she had made it her duty to be the first one there in the morning and the last one to leave in the evening and the only one on Saturday and Sunday.

She slipped out of her bed, ignoring the cold seeping in through the open bedroom window. She grabbed her running clothes from the hook on the door, hurried into them and left the room to put on her running shoes in the hallway. Neither the clothes nor the shoes were modern or new; the clothes had even started to show little tears, but Michaela did not care. The tears did not impact the functionality of the piece of clothing, so it would have been a waste to replace them with new ones.

She firmly tied the laces of her shoes and ran down the stairs. Outside, she collided with a cloud of her own breath. It was even colder than the day before. She jumped up and down a few times and rubbed her hands over her arms trying to warm up. After some stretching, she started to run. She would never have considered joining a fitness club or buying training equipment. All of that would have cost money and was, as far as she was concerned, completely superfluous. The forest was just a few steps away, and it did not cost a penny.

Exactly thirty minutes later, she returned. Shortly thereafter, she drove her car across town, through streets that were decorated for the holidays, but still devoid of other people. She could not stop calculating the electric bill for all of those lights. Thank god, she did not have to pay for it. Nevertheless, it was wasted money.

She also considered it a waste to drive to work in her own car. She would have preferred to use public transportation, which would have been much cheaper. However, it seemed that was only meant for people who worked half days, from eight or eight-thirty in the morning to four in the afternoon and not at all on the weekends. The bus schedules did not support regular working days, from six in the morning to ten or twelve at night, seven days a week. Michaela was not surprised the economy was faltering, with people working so little time.

And, to top it off, they always demanded more and more money. A vacation bonus, a holiday bonus, sick pay – Michaela shuddered. The unbelievable audacity! She never took advantage of any of those privileges for herself. Should they not be glad just to be employed?

She entered the company building and enjoyed, in her own detached way, the peace that emanated from the empty rooms. At times, she felt almost disturbed when her employees finally arrived, after she had been working away for hours. If they came that late, why did they bother to come at all?

She sat down behind her desk and pulled from her briefcase the files that she had taken home the previous night to work on – before she found Karina. She was still upset about that ambush. What had followed ... oh well. Karina undoubtedly was talented between the sheets. Still, she had stolen a few hours of her valuable night rest, and Michaela doubted her efforts could fully compensate for that.

Short-term excitement and relaxation, was it really worth it? Could she put a price on it? No. So why did she not stay away from it altogether?

"Good Morning, Ms. Wittling. Coffee?" Her secretary smiled at her.

"I don't need coffee." Michaela looked up indignantly.

"It doesn't cost you anything. It's being paid for with money from the coffee fund, to which we all contribute." Her secretary tried to hide a grin.

"I don't want any gifts from anybody," Michaela growled and concentrated again on her files.

"Then pour it down the drain." Her secretary placed a steaming coffee cup next to her.

"Mrs. Majakowski." Michaela stared at her. "How many times have I told you not to do this?"

Mrs. Majakowski continued to smile. "Every day. But you won't stop me. I'll retire in ten years. Then you'll be rid of me."

"You'll probably even instruct your successor to continue this way," Michaela grumbled.

"Probably," Mrs. Majakowski replied cheerfully. "I know you won't dump out the coffee, you're much too . . . frugal for that."

"I think 'cheap' is the word you were looking for."

"No, I wasn't. Nevertheless, I've known you for so long now. Ms. Wittling, I knew you when you were a child. Please permit me to have some motherly feelings."

"Motherly feelings?" Michaela's head snapped up.

"I'm sorry. I didn't mean it that way." Evelyn Majakowski turned serious. "I know, your mother —"

"My mother was a whore." Michaela's voice was distant and cool while she thumbed through her files and added notes here and there.

"Ms. Wittling, don't be so hard on others . . . and on yourself. Your mother enjoyed life. Just like your father. I don't approve of her abandoning you like that, but she was . . . she was not made for this kind of life."

"I think what you meant to say is that she was not made for a life without my grandfather's money." Michaela gave a hollow laugh. "Of course, she expected much more from being married to the heir of Wittling & Co."

"Many people who grow up with humble means put too much value on money," Mrs. Majakowski said. "You can't fault them for it. They never learned differently."

Michaela snorted. "You don't need to sugarcoat anything. I know what happened. My mother was a floozy. My father picked her up somewhere, and then he knocked her up. More likely, she was out to get pregnant by him – guided by the gleam of the money she was expecting. And when I was born, and she found out that there was none to get, she just disappeared."

"It's never easy to give up a child. I'm sure it wasn't easy for your mother either. She knew you'd have a good life."

"And that's why she took off? You're too sentimental, Mrs. Majakowski. Face it; she couldn't care less about me. She was only in it for the money." Michaela got up and went to the file cabinet, her face showing no signs of emotion.

Mrs. Majakowski shook her head with regret and left Michaela's office.

"Am I too late?" Ramona hurried down the corridor.

"A little bit." Mrs. Majakowski looked at her watch.

"I was needed at the hospital –"

"I know." Evelyn Majakowski interrupted her. "You always are. We all understand . . . more than understand." She looked at Ramona with compassion.

"I assume she doesn't." Ramona tilted her head towards Michaela's office. "I'm always afraid she might fire me because I come late so often or have to leave in the middle of the day."

Mrs. Majakowski gave her a small smile. "She doesn't know. And she will never know. I keep track of everyone's hours."

"And if she ever finds out?" Ramona asked with trepidation. "I don't want you to get in trouble over me."

"I won't. Even if . . . I know how to handle her. I know her well enough." Evelyn Majakowski placed a hand on Ramona's arm and smiled encouragingly. "Now calm down. Go grab a cup of coffee. Work's not going anywhere."

స్తున్న

ould you have time now to speak with the representatives from the children's charity?" Mrs. Majakowski poked her head through the door to Michaela's office.

"Children's charity?" Michaela frowned. "What is that supposed to be?"

"A charitable organization that helps children." Mrs. Majakowski opened the door wide. "Please come in. Ms. Wittling has time for you now."

"I don't have –!" Michaela jumped up from behind her desk, but Evelyn Majakowski was already gone, and in her place two bundled-up people were standing in the room, a woman and a man.

The man approached Michaela with an outstretched hand. "Ms. Wittling. I'm pleased to finally meet you in person."

I can't say the same, Michaela thought, accepting the handshake only reluctantly.

The older woman loosened her scarf and opened the top button of her coat before she, too, extended her hand in greeting. "I can still remember your father – and your grandfather," she said with a smile. "It was always a joy to meet with him. He gave from his heart."

"Oh, that's what it's about." Michaela sat down. "You want a donation."

"There was a tradition in the Wittling Company to –"

"When my grandfather was still running the company – and my father," Michaela interrupted the man. "I have not subscribed to this tradition."

"It's Christmas . . ."

"Oh, is it already?" Michaela swiveled around in her chair and looked at the big wall calendar, a present from one of their suppliers. "I hadn't noticed. Times never change for me. All days are the same."

"But, Christmas . . ." the man stammered.

"It's not possible to miss out on Christmas, you mean?" Michaela gave the man an ironic smile that did not reach her eyes. "You are absolutely right. It's an unfathomable extravagance. Everything is brightly illuminated, day and night. I don't want to know the cost of all of that."

"Christmas is only once a year." The older woman tried to support her colleague. "And it's the most important holiday of all, particularly for children. We try to bring joy to those children whose parents can't afford to give them presents or those who don't even have parents anymore. Many companies donate something from their own product lines –"

Michaela's laugh sounded almost sincere. "Wine and liquor! Those are my product lines. Hopefully you don't want to suggest I donate some of that to the children?"

"No, no." The woman smiled. "That would not be appropriate, of course."

"Well, there you are." Michaela got up from her chair. "I can't really donate anything. That would be that then."

"But –" The man and the woman were perplexed. The woman was the first to regain her composure. "Your grandfather always –"

"I know what my grandfather did." Michaela raised a hand. "But I can't afford those kinds of expenses. Under my grandfather, the business flourished and the profits were good. Today, however, there's hardly any profit to be made. Taxes, fees, personnel expenses, declining sales figures, you are probably aware of the current economic situation. I have to be glad I can afford to run the business."

"Donations are tax deductible." The man sounded desperate now.

"That doesn't mean they will be reimbursed. They only lower the profit. And, if there is no profit, it can't be lowered. So there would be no tax benefit."

The two charity representatives were stunned into silence.

"And, by the way," Michaela continued, "whatever happened to good old public welfare?"

"Social welfare, you mean," the man squeezed out the words through white lips.

"Yes, that's what I mean. Isn't that what's driving our country into ruins? Too much social spending? So, everybody is taken care of nicely, it seems."

"It's about the children," the woman said in a pleading tone. "The poorest of the poor. There are also many people who are too proud to accept welfare. And then it's again the children who suffer. They can't apply for it themselves, you know."

"Then they should start learning to," Michaela said. "Or wait until they earn their own money."

"If they'll still be able to by then," the man said. He put on his gloves. "Come on, Linda, it's no use. I wouldn't even have come, but you always said that old Wittling —"

"That old Mr. Wittling was a generous man, a great person," the woman replied. "That's what I remembered. I had forgotten that's not necessarily been passed onto the next generation."

They left the room without attempting to shake Michaela's hand once more.

After a few minutes, Evelyn Majakowski entered the office. "You didn't give anything?"

Michaela had already forgotten about her visitors. "What? Oh, right." She looked up from her papers. "As far as I know, I wouldn't get anything for donating something. What would be my return on investment?"

"Peace of mind," Evelyn Majakowski said.

"Peace of mind?" Michaela raised an amused eyebrow. "My mind — and the rest of me — is at peace, don't you worry. I sleep very well at night."

"That surprises me," Evelyn Majakowski commented. She sighed.

She usually did not justify her actions, but Michaela felt the need to explain her reasoning to the woman who had known her since childhood. "You knew my father," she said. "You know what a squanderer he was. He ruined the company. I have inherited the extravagance of both my parents. That's why I have to be careful. I could end up like them."

"I don't believe that for one moment, Michaela." Evelyn Majakowski had not used Michaela's first name in a long time; she sounded highly skeptical. "I don't think you are susceptible to excess. If you were, you'd have shown signs of it by now."

"My father's compulsive gambling runs through my blood," Michaela said. "I noticed it once. I've never gambled since, and I won't ever again."

"That only proves me right," Evelyn Majakowski said and smiled. "You don't need to be afraid. Your father had no self-control, but you do. You are not your father." She gave Michaela a stern look. "Maybe your self-control is too rigid at times. Stinginess can be just as compulsive as extravagance."

"I'd rather be stingy than wasteful," Michaela retorted defiantly.

"You won't go bankrupt if you allocate the money sensibly, including donations," Evelyn countered. "What you give to others will come back to you a thousand fold."

Michaela shook her head in disagreement. "I had no idea you were such an idealist, Mrs. Majakowski."

"When you were a child, Ms. Wittling," Evelyn returned to the formal address, "didn't you like to celebrate Christmas, sitting by the Christmas tree and enjoying your presents?"

"I can barely remember that time," Michaela growled.

"But you do," her secretary insisted. "And now? Don't you think you would enjoy sitting by the tree again with somebody and not just being there by yourself?"

"I don't have a Christmas tree," Michaela grumbled.

"Maybe you would have one then," her secretary replied dryly.

"I have no idea what you are trying to say — and I don't even want to know!" Michaela got impatient now.

"You know exactly what I mean. It's not good to be alone. That's even in the bible." It took all of Evelyn's energy to stay calm. Michaela was really behaving like a little child.

"Another one of those superfluous things!" Michaela looked at Evelyn. "Now, is that all?" She wanted to get rid of Evelyn as fast as possible. It was starting to get to her. First those beggars and now her secretary. She had a lot of work to do, and everybody was keeping her from it with these discussions.

"It's late already," Evelyn said, as if to hint at something. But Michaela didn't catch on. "It's Christmas Eve. We are the only ones still here. Everybody else has left; though, Ms. Benckhoff is coming back later. You know, she's going to finish the year-end accounting."

Michaela nodded, clearly not listening to her. She just wanted to be left alone.

Evelyn Majakowski sighed deeply. "Merry Christmas, Michaela," she said in a soft voice and closed the door behind her.

❧ ❦ ❧ ❦

C an I go home with you, Mommy?" Leonie asked, her eyes shining.

Ramona was sitting at Leonie's hospital bed and almost started to cry when she heard these words.

"I want to go home for Christmas."

Ramona swallowed. She could not show her daughter how she was feeling. She tried to smile. "Not this year, sweetheart," she said. "You see the IV and all that? It would be much too difficult to take that home. Our apartment is too small. There's not enough room for all of it."

Leonie made a face. "Do we have to take all of it with us? Can't we just leave it here?"

Ramona tried to decide if she should lie to her daughter or tell her the truth. Maybe it would be better if she knew — but she was still so young. How was she supposed to understand this? "No, we can't," she said quietly and smiled. "You need it all, so you won't feel bad again, like a few days ago. You don't want to feel bad, do you?" She carefully brushed the hair from her daughter's forehead. "But when you feel better, you'll come home, and we'll celebrate Christmas then, for sure."

"Promise?"

"Promise." Ramona struggled to keep her composure. She felt like collapsing on the bed and giving in to her tears. "I have to go now," she said. "To work. I'll be back tomorrow. You'll probably be up and running around by then and teasing Florian."

"He teases me!" Leonie's little face was haggard, showing signs of fever, but she still had enough energy to protest.

"Of course. He teases you." Ramona put on her most confident smile. She bent down and kissed her daughter's cheeks, which were gleaming and wet with sweat.

When she stepped out into the corridor, she steadied herself against the wall. Then she slowly straightened. Maybe it was good after all that she could go to work now. She would not have to think of Leonie constantly, of what was lying ahead for her. For a few seconds, she would not see her little face in front of her, how she got smaller and smaller, weaker and weaker.

᧞᧞᧞᧞᧞

Ms. Wittling? Would you have a moment for me?"

Michaela's head snapped up. She had completely forgotten that there was somebody else in the office, despite Mrs. Majakowski's announcement. "Yes?"

Ramona entered the dark room. There was only a small desk lamp that illuminated a tiny part of Michaela's desktop. *Even here she's saving,* Ramona thought. "I have a question about the accounts. Usually I wouldn't bother you with it, but –"

"Get on with it!" Michaela was already growing impatient again. "What is it?"

"This receipt . . ." Ramona walked over to Michaela's desk and tried to hold the paper into the tiny beam of Michaela's lamp. "It's simply wrong. I checked the warehouse. We had ordered one hundred bottles of champagne, and that's also what the invoice says. But they only delivered ten bottles."

"Beg your pardon?" Michaela stared at her.

"Yes, it's true," Ramona confirmed.

"Has the invoice been paid yet?" Michaela now stared at the piece of paper.

"Yes, unfortunately. Apparently, nobody made the effort to look. When the delivery came, the number was just checked off."

"Ten instead of one hundred?" Michaela could not fathom it.

"Yes. To be honest, I don't understand it either. But we definitely got only ten bottles, that's for sure."

"This is the most expensive champagne we have,"

Michaela said.

"Yes," Ramona confirmed again. One bottle cost more than she earned in a month – in several months.

Michaela got up and started pacing the room. "I don't believe that was an accident," she mumbled to herself.

"You think somebody stole them?"

"What? Yes." Michaela answered absentmindedly. She had already forgotten that Ramona was in the room. "I'll get to the bottom of this," she said through clenched teeth. She sat down. "Thank you very much for pointing it out to me. Have you found any more irregularities?"

"None so far," Ramona said. "It's the first time I noticed something like this. But I'm not through with everything."

"OK." Michaela bent low over her desk to be able to use the small light source.

"Oh, Ms. Wittling?"

Michaela looked up with an irritated expression. She could hardly see Ramona in the dark of the room. "What is it?"

"I . . . I wanted to apologize for coming so late. I was at the hospital."

"At the hospital? Are you sick?" Michaela's questions sounded indifferent.

"No, I'm not. But my daughter."

Michaela nodded automatically. "She'll get better," she stated, uninterested. "Children often have something."

Ramona felt the tears stinging in her eyes. "My daughter is dying, Ms. Wittling," she replied with a wavering voice, "and there's nothing I can do about it." Then she hurried out of the room.

A short time later Michaela heard the heavy front door falling closed.

❧ ❦ ❧ ❦ ❧

It was late when Michaela headed home that evening. The streets were deserted. She entered her apartment where everything looked exactly as it always did. There were no Christmas decorations, no burning candles. Michaela missed none of it. What was all that humbug for anyway?

The apartment had only sparse furnishing; there was nothing unnecessary. Michaela's idea of superfluous included a coffee machine, a refrigerator and a television. She had none of those.

She had moved into the apartment with the few pieces of furniture remaining from the previous tenant. She had been forced to sell her family's house after she had inherited the company and discovered that she was nearly bankrupt. Her father had needed only a few months to ruin what had taken her grandfather decades and a lot of effort to build. At that moment, she had taken a solemn oath never to become like her father. Yes, he had always been everybody's darling. However, Michaela was not after that. Popularity had no value. Money was the only thing that counted, never having to rely on anybody.

She crossed her apartment in the weak light streaming through the window from a street lamp. Why should she turn on a light? She knew where everything was. There was hardly any furniture, so there was not much opportunity to run into anything. She did not have to pay for the street lamp – although, that was not entirely true either, her taxes paid for it, much to her annoyance.

She just wanted to change out of her clothes, brush her teeth and fall into her bed. She had no use for Christmas.

She did not notice that the light through the window seemed to be brighter that night because the street lamp was supported by the many colored lights shining out from the surrounding windows. Had she noticed, she would not have cared. At worst, she would have gotten upset about people's wastefulness. Those people somehow felt the need to illuminate the street, which was a waste if they were inside.

She yawned and went to bed, shivering when her body hit the cold sheets. There was no heat in her bedroom. It would get warm under the blanket in a moment, as always. She was still waiting for all of her toes to adjust to the surrounding temperature when she started to drift off.

She had a strange dream. What was even stranger: She usually did not dream at all. While she was dreaming, she was not aware of that, of course.

She was running through a long corridor, searching for something, though she would not have been able to say what exactly she was looking for. She opened every door, of which there were incredibly many on the seemingly endless corridor, and looked inside. She found herself in front of storage rooms, bricked-up doors and windows, never finding what she was searching for. Once there seemed to be a room flooded with light behind one door, but when she wanted to look inside to see what kind of room it was, the door closed, and she was back in the dimly lit corridor. She noticed she was starting to panic. She knew, she had to find it ... it ... it ... whatever it was.

"Mike ... Mike ..." A voice drifted through her dream. "Mike ..."

She opened her eyes and peered into the darkness. Her

bedroom faced the courtyard; not even the street lamps could cast a glow here. Still, her eyes adjusted quickly to the absence of light, and it was as if shadows populated the room, formless, faceless shadows.

"Mike . . ."

It sounded like an echo, a faraway echo without any substance, as if coming from nowhere, as if it had no origin.

Michaela set up straight in her bed. It could not be that she was just imagining this! She had never had nightmares. There had to be some real cause. A burglar maybe?

She scanned the room – as much as she could see. She was not prepared for a situation like this. To be honest, she had always thought there was nothing to steal in her apartment – which was probably true – and that she could neglect any kind of security. She had an ordinary lock on her front door. That was it. She had no weapons, neither for defense nor for offense. She knew her grandfather had had a pistol, a souvenir from the war, and she knew that pistol still had to be somewhere. But, even if she were to find it, it was not likely that it would still fire.

A flashlight on her bedside table would have been very useful now. It would have provided light, and she could have used it as a weapon. Unfortunately, Michaela had thought that investment was unnecessary too.

She lay down again and tried to calm herself. She could hear the sound of her own breathing and her rapidly pounding heart. With difficulty, she tried to get both into a slower rhythm.

A rustle. She held her breath. She knew there had to be something in the room.

She stared into the darkness, unable to move. The little bit of light in the room seemed to change, as if suddenly a street lamp was switched on outside. This could not have been, after all, there were no street lamps in the courtyard.

No, the light did not come from outside, it came from inside. Michaela sat up again; and this time she got out of bed. If there was something there, she wanted to face it upright. The air was freezing, but she did not feel it, even though her feet tried to call her attention to it.

"Mike ..." One of the formless shadows glided towards her.

Michaela shrank back, startled, but then stopped. She was hallucinating; that was all.

The shadow hovered in the air in front of her and then suddenly took shape – a female shape. A face peeled itself out of the darkness, strangely familiar and unfamiliar at the same time. Suddenly Michaela recognized something very familiar. "Karina?"

The shadow with Karina's shape smiled.

Michaela took a deep breath. What was that woman thinking? "Did you use your key again, even though I told you not to?" she asked with irritation in her voice. Then she scowled. Had she not taken the key from Karina?

With an unusual expression on her face, rather angelically innocent and a small halo around her head, Karina answered, "I didn't need to. Not this time." She smiled a shadowy smile.

Michaela wanted to say something but shut her mouth again right away. She was confused, because Karina was so different. She did not know her like this. "Why are you here, in the middle of the night?" she asked when the shadow did not seem to want to move.

"It is a very special night," Karina whispered, the angel-ic smile still on her face.

"It is a very cold night!" Michaela snapped. Suddenly she became aware of the frostbite threatening her bare feet standing on the bare floor. She fumbled for her slip-pers and put them on. Unfortunately, they were also cold.

"It's as cold a night as it has to be," Karina said. "As it always is."

"Why are you out and about then? Don't you have a bed at home?" A knowing smile spread over Michaela's face. "Or is your bed empty? Are you alone and looking for company?" Now she knew what was up. She recalled that Karina could not stand being alone. Her bed was rarely empty. And today – on Christmas – all of her lov-ers were busy elsewhere – all except Michaela. So Kari-na had come over.

"You are the one looking for something, not I," said Karina.

Michaela remembered her dream. "How do you –?" She started to feel spooked.

"I know everything," Karina replied, "but there's a lot that you don't know yet – or no longer. That's why you will have visitors tonight."

"What? More visitors? Do you want to have an orgy?" Michaela laughed.

"You just don't understand," Karina said. "I'm not the one you think I am. I'm just a messenger."

"I rather think you're a bad dream caused by my upset stomach," Michaela replied. "Or you're playing a trick on me." She waved her hand dismissively. "Leave me alone. I have to sleep. It'll be morning soon, and I have to go to work." She crawled into her bed and pulled the blanket up over her shoulders. My god, that was cold!

"Tomorrow can wait," Karina said, "but you might not."

"Don't talk in riddles!" Michaela got upset. "That's not your style." Indeed, Karina was the most direct person she knew. She never hid what she wanted. Why was she doing it now?

"You are capable of making even an apparition like me sigh," Karina said. "You don't believe in what you see. You walk through the world with your eyes shut, without looking around you. Do you never stop?"

"Stop and smell the roses, you mean?" Michaela laughed with chattering teeth as she shivered under her blanket. "Are you Satan offering me a single moment that's so beautiful I'd want it to last forever in exchange for the world?" She propped herself up. "All right, make me an offer. I'll think about it."

"I'm not the devil." Karina glided away. "Like I said, I'm just a messenger. The others will come. Be ready."

"The others? What others?" Michaela stared confused into the darkness that started to spread out again. The light coming from Karina's shape waned. "What others?" Michaela yelled into the silence that followed the darkness.

But there was no reply.

❧❧❧❧

S he woke to the tolling of a bell. A bell? Not fully awake yet, she knit her brows. Where did that bell come from? She had never heard one before. The next church tower was miles away; and besides, the bells were not rung at night so they would not disturb anybody's sleep. They would not be rung again until six —

Six o'clock? With a jerk, she sat up straight as a candle in her bed. Had she overslept? Six o'clock already?

She listened to the tolls. She had not counted the first few, but she counted now. It seemed there were more than six.

"Correct, correct . . . there are twelve." A soft cackling voice could be heard from the darkness.

Michaela looked around wildly, stared into the chasm of the night. "Karina?"

Again, a soft cackle could be heard. "The messenger has gone and won't come back again. Did she not announce me?" The voice sounded a tad insulted.

Michaela still tried to figure out who was speaking. There was nothing to see. "Announced? Who are you?"

"Oh, well. It's always the same." The darkness slowly turned into light. It started in the middle of something that looked like a red tunnel. Then, the circle got bigger. The tunnel expanded. The light turned yellow, then white, and then a small figure stepped out, eagerly rubbing its hands together. "I always have to do everything myself. There I go, sending out the heralds to prepare people and what do they do? Simply don't say anything." It shook its head.

"She . . . she did say something," Michaela stammered. "She announced a visitor. Is that you?" It was a dream, surely; it had to be a dream. This could not be real. Michaela shook her head, tried to pinch her arm.

"You are awake," the figure said. "Don't worry; it's the same with almost everybody." He shook his head again. "Visitor, visitor! Could she not have been a bit more precise? She had exact orders –" He interrupted himself and sighed. "Okay. I guess I will have to do the rest of the work. I really had hoped I was spared it this time."

"What? What work?" Michaela stared at the little creature that bore no resemblance to anything she had ever seen. In fact, it seemed to change shape constantly. It grew, then shrank. It was a man, then a woman, a child, a dwarf, a giant – she simply could not determine what it really was.

"Listen up. I'll give you the short version." The little man – or girl or whatever – rubbed its hands together again. "You are not very nice to your fellow human beings."

Michaela's mouth fell open. "I'm not . . . nice? You came all the way here to tell me that?" She almost laughed.

"Yeah well, there's cause and effect, right?" The creature gave her a punishing look. "One leads to the other."

Michaela got a grip on herself again. "Just a moment ago you were upset at Karina for not telling me everything, and now you're doing the same: You are talking in riddles."

"Riddles, riddles!" The figure flung up its hands. "Everything's always a riddle for you folks! As if it's that difficult!" Patience did not seem to be this creature's forte.

That was something Michaela knew well. She could

deal with that. "Then explain it to me," she said, "or leave. I'm too late already anyway. Or —" She glanced around, but she had no alarm clock. "Twelve, you said?"

"The time of day doesn't matter," the creature said.

"It matters to me," Michaela said. "When I went to bed it was past midnight. Is the night already over? But then it would have to be day. Or night again. But I can't have slept that long."

"You slept as long as you had to sleep," the little man said. "And now don't interrupt me with such nonsense. I'm not here for that."

Michaela laughed. "But it seems you also won't tell me exactly why you are here. All right, I got the message: I'm not nice to my fellow human beings. Can I go back to sleep now?" Michaela snuggled into her sheets.

"GRRRRRTTTTT!" A terrible noise came from the back corner, increased and then rang through the air and reverberated in Michaela's ears.

"Hey now, are you done yet?" Michaela sat up outraged. "This is my bedroom. You have no business being here. Get lost already! And, by the way, you are just a bad dream anyway. I must have eaten something wrong. But it'll pass. Like gas."

"Gas? Gas? You think I'm flatulence?" The little man danced around in front of her and waved his arms. "You really are a hopeless case. I'm not even sure anymore why I'm here." The little guy stomped an invisible foot on the floor. The whole house shook.

"My goodness, calm down, will you!" Michaela jumped out of her bed and put her hands on her hips. "You invade my privacy, wake me up, keep me from falling asleep, give a useless speech, and then you're complaining that I won't take you seriously? I don't even know who or what you are!"

"I'm the Ghost of Christmas Past," the little man said, suddenly well mannered.

"What?" Michaela stared at him.

"The Ghost of Christmas Past," the little man repeated. "You asked me to introduce myself."

"The Ghost of Christmas Past?" Michaela asked. "What's that supposed to be?"

"You'll see. Come on, now." The little guy walked over to the window.

"Come? Where?" Michaela looked bewildered at the audacious creature that now threw her bedroom window wide open. In this cold!

"You'll see," the ghost insisted. "And I hope it will be of good use to you."

"Good use?" Michaela had regained part of her composure. "Sleeping would be a good use of my time! But you're stealing it from me. You couldn't be more useless if you tried!"

At the end of the ghost's arm a hand appeared. It grew longer and longer until it grabbed Michaela's arm and pulled her to the window.

Michaela stiffened, because the ghost was already floating out the window. "Wait! I can't fly!" she yelled. "And I'm only in my pajamas! I'll catch my death!"

"Death appears in many forms," the ghost replied. "Some are already dead while they are still alive, while they are walking and breathing. But I can assure you, your death won't be coming this way, as you fear. You can trust me."

Michaela knew that trust was the last feeling she had towards this apparition, as her feet lost contact with the floor, and she was pulled through the window into the silence of Christmas Eve. No device was visible that could have held her suspended in the air. She simply floated.

She stared down, saw the street below. The light from the lanterns sparkled in the snow and illuminated it in a way she had never seen before. It was a golden shimmer that turned ice into amber, into silver and ivory.

That only lasted a moment, and then suddenly everything around her changed and it was daylight. She gently floated down into a snow-covered garden, where a happily smiling snowman stood guard. They landed behind a tree. Michaela's feet seemed to touch the ground again, but even though they were bare and the earth had a blanket of snow, she did not feel the cold. She remained unaffected by the weather, as if she were wrapped in a cocoon.

"Do you know this house?" the ghost asked while Michaela was still pondering why she could not feel the cold.

She lifted her gaze. "That's my grandfather's house," she said. "Our house. I grew up here."

She felt what was almost a gentle caress, like the memory of long lost hopes and expectations, of things she had wished for but that had never happened.

"There, look," the ghost said; its voice sounded as if it was not spoken into Michaela's ears but coming from deep within her, from her heart. "The children are coming home from school."

A boisterous group approached on the path that led to the house with the garden where Michaela was standing. Colorful scarves blew over checkered parkas and thick winter coats, hats fell into the snow because they could not cling to the bouncing heads of the excited children.

Even the heavy packs on the children's backs did not seem able to put a damper on their happiness and keep them down.

One child, a little girl, broke from the group and hurried towards the house.

"Merry Christmas!" came shouts from her friends.

"Merry Christmas!" the little girl called back and laughed before impatiently pushing open the gate and plowing through the snow as she crossed the garden.

"Now, now, slow down," said a man between chuckles as he stepped out of the house. "Hold your horses!"

"Grandfather!" The girl rejoiced and ran into the man's open arms. "When is Christmas? We've been let out of school today, so it has to be Christmas soon, isn't that right?"

The man laughed again and threw the girl high into the air catching her as she giggled with joy. "It is Christmas, my dear. Now we'll put up the tree, and then Santa Claus can come. He won't come if we don't have a pretty tree. So we'll have to work extra hard on the decorations."

"Yes, Grandfather." The girl's voice sounded devout. "We will."

"Come on." The man set the girl down and lovingly took her hand. "First you'll get some hot soup, and then we'll get started."

They went into the house, and the door closed with a soft click, as if it did not want to disturb the wintry silence that had settled once again over the garden.

"Do you remember?" the ghost asked.

Michaela's head jerked up as if she were being torn from deepest thought. "Of course, I remember," she replied defensively, "but that was a long time ago. My grandfather was still alive."

"A shadow from the past, you're right," the ghost said gently. "But often the past is not as much in the past as we think."

"I'm not a child anymore!" Michaela snapped. "What's this nonsense all about?"

"Christmas time is a cheerful time," the ghost replied, "for children as well as adults." As if to confirm his words, the clear winter air filled with children's laughter, permeating everything, leaving no stone untouched. "Cheerfulness and love everywhere, that's what Christmas is all about."

"Merry Christmas, ha!" Michaela tried to turn away but cheerfulness seemed to be all around her, beaming down from the clouds, unwilling to be pushed aside. "What do I get out of all of this? The only useful thing is business. Business is good around the holidays — much better than the rest of the year. And it's really great at New Year's with everybody drinking sparkling wine and champagne. But that's all there is to it. There is no other meaning to Christmas."

"Business? That's all Christmas is to you? Good business?" The ghost shook its head.

"That's all it is to everybody who owns a business," Michaela said. "Just look at the displays in the stores at Christmas. Do you really think storeowners do that out of the sheer goodness of their hearts? To bring joy to the people? A good business sense, that's all there is to it."

"On the surface, maybe," the ghost said with a deep sigh. "But when everybody's at home, sitting by the Christmas tree, don't you think that's something else?"

"I don't have a Christmas tree!" Michaela repeated stubbornly.

"I know." The ghost sighed again. This was proving to be a difficult case, a very difficult case. "Come on. Let's keep going."

"Going? Where?" Michaela looked at him, unwilling to continue. "How much longer are you planning to keep me?"

"You're not losing any time," the ghost said. "Time has no meaning here. Let's find out what else there is to see."

Suddenly, day turned into night. They were standing in a room full of candles, in front of a Christmas tree that seemed to fill the whole room with light, even the ceiling. Light reflected off the round ornaments hanging from the branches where figures danced on top threatening to fall off at any minute, and soft music played in the background.

Two men, one older and one younger, were sitting in deep leather chairs. The younger man was not so young. He seemed to be past his prime. They resembled each other, but where the older man's strong chin indicated assertiveness and good judgment, the younger man's spongy cheeks and red nose betrayed his excessive and unstable lifestyle.

"What's holding her up?" the younger man asked with a glance at the door.

"She'll be here soon. Young girls tend to need a lot of time," the older man said gently.

In that moment, the door opened, and a young woman entered the room.

The older man jumped to his feet. "You look wonderful," he said, admiring her slender figure as the young woman walked into the middle of the room.

The younger man turned in his chair. "Beautiful," he

confirmed. "You look just like –" He was interrupted by a stern look from the older man. "It's incredible," he continued after clearing his throat. "I haven't seen you in a year, and now you're already a proper young lady."

"Maybe you should come by more often, father," the young woman said with coolness in her voice. "My appearance might not surprise you so much then."

"I had things to do," Michaela's father said. "I was away on business."

Michaela's younger self looked at the spent face in front of her. "I can see that," she said.

"It's Christmas, let's not argue," Michaela's grandfather interrupted. "This is a peaceful time."

"I have no intention of picking a fight," young Michaela said. She smiled. This smile would surely have surprised everybody who knew her these days. It spread across her face, lighting up her features. "Hermione cooked a fantastic goose, and you'll have to be fast to get some."

"Yeah, sure, you want to have it all to yourself." Her grandfather laughed and linked arms with her. "I'd like to watch you try."

Michaela's father got out of the chair. The young woman held out her other arm to him in a conciliatory gesture. "Let's go eat, father," she said with a smile.

"Yes, let's." Her father slid his arm around hers, and the three of them, young Michaela in the middle, walked to the dining room.

Michaela watched this scene, wanting to hold on to this glimpse into the past. She stretched her neck as if to try to see more but the image faded, and a different one appeared.

They were on the street now, in the city. People were hustling and bustling down the sidewalks past store windows that showed off illuminated decorations, golden angels and boxes wrapped in colored paper. The street itself was illuminated so brightly that it looked like daytime, though beyond the glare was the dark of night. Michaela recognized that it was the street leading to her company, but it seemed to be a different time. People were not wearing modern clothes.

Michaela frowned. "I left my office not that long ago," she said. "You won't be able to show me anything there that I don't know or that I don't remember."

"It's not the same office that you left," the ghost said. "Look."

They stood in front of the glass entrance doors to the offices of Wittling & Co. Through the milky glass one could see that inside all the lights were on, colors in all shades of the rainbow spread throughout the room.

Michaela grimaced. "I gave orders to only switch on the lights needed for work," she said. "Who has the impertinence to –?"

In this moment, the door was pushed open and laughing people stepped outside. "I never want to work anywhere else," a young man announced cheerfully. "The boss knows how to celebrate Christmas."

"Come on, let's hurry up and find that wine in the cellar that he wants," the young woman replied. "I don't want to miss too much of the party."

"Yes, let's hurry!" The two laughed and ran off, down the hallway.

Michaela hesitated. They entered the offices and were greeted by happy chatter and cheers. Bursts of laughter kept interrupting the overlapping conversations. The tables were laden with wine bottles and plates piled high with hors d'oeuvres and pastries from the buffet stretching down one wall of the room. Between traditional Christmas tunes, there was music for dancing, and everyone got into the rhythm.

One couple danced towards Michaela and the ghost. Michaela wanted to get out of the way, but her companion held her back. "We're not here and neither are they. We're all just shadows."

Michaela gulped when the couple came closer. It was her grandfather and she, dancing in a good mood and laughing at each other. "I just love it when people are happy," her grandfather said. "Is there anything better than celebrating after working hard all year?"

"It is astonishing how you do this every year," said young Michaela in his arms, looking rather grown-up already. "I've never seen anything like it. Not even at the university."

"How is university?" her grandfather asked. "Do you like it there?"

"Sadly, business administration is mostly dry numbers." Young Michaela frowned. "But I wanted to do it, so why shouldn't I like it?" She gave her grandfather a big smile.

"Good for you, my child," her grandfather said with a proud smile. "You seem to be just like me. Your father ..." His expression darkened slightly as his eyes looked to a different corner of the room where Michaela's father, showing signs of having too much wine, swayed in the arms of a female employee.

At that moment, Evelyn Majakowski – a decidedly younger Evelyn Majakowski – came by and held a collection tin out to young Michaela and her grandfather. "Alms for the poor, alms for the poor," she sang and flashed a big smile at them.

Michaela's grandfather chuckled and ended the dance. "It's still not enough? I know how much I have already given."

"That's already been used up," Evelyn Majakowski said with an impish wink. "Second helpings, please . . ."

"All right, if I have to . . ." Michaela's grandfather chuckled again and pulled out his wallet. He took out a big banknote, rolled it up and squeezed it into the collection tin. "It's for a good cause after all. You can never do too much in that respect."

"Hear, hear." Evelyn Majakowski thanked him with a polite curtsy, as if standing on stage, and continued dancing and singing through the room to entice everybody to donate more.

"You're already paying for everything," Michaela said. "Why doesn't she quit bugging you?"

"Why should she?" Her grandfather grinned. "I gave her that job. So, I have to lead by good example. You should never demand others do something if you're not willing to do the same."

"You already give so much," Michaela said and looked lovingly at her grandfather.

"You can never give too much," her grandfather said. "We are so fortunate. I want the whole world to be as fortunate as we are, at least on Christmas."

"You are an incorrigible idealist." Michaela laughed and lightly tapped her grandfather's chin. "One would never know you're a business man."

"That's why I never spend more than I have and don't create any debt," her grandfather said. "Once you take over the company, I hope you'll keep it that way."

"Oh, I will," Michaela said. "Definitely."

The scene dissolved.

"So, do you think your grandfather took out a loan and ended up with debt to give this party?" the ghost asked.

"Debt?" Michaela was aghast. "No. He did as he always said. Never create debt. That party wasn't so expensive, it was no big deal."

"No big deal ..." the ghost repeated as if mulling it over. "Why then was everybody so excited and happy? Why did everybody praise and thank him so much? Was it really worth it?"

"Was it worth it? Was my grandfather worth it?" Michaela repeated furiously. "It wasn't about the money. They didn't love him for his money. It was the atmosphere, they felt appreciated, they were not just thankful for the party. It was his way of showing his appreciation for them, for their work, their dedication and loyalty to the company. The joy they derived from each other was no match for the rather small financial expense. It's the small things that count, not the sum. It's the personal, the involvement; no money in the world can make up for that."

Michaela had talked herself into a fury, but when she finished, she noticed that the ghost was not saying anything and just staring at her.

"What?" she asked grumpily. "Suddenly you don't have anything to say? You haven't been at a loss for words yet, unfortunately."

"I think you already said everything," the ghost replied.

"If you think so," Michaela mumbled. "My grandfather was the best man in the world. You'll never get me to say anything bad about him."

"I wouldn't want to," the ghost said. "But, let's hurry now. I want to show you something else."

"You already showed me enough," Michaela said. "I've

about had it. I want to go back to bed and sleep."

But her objections did not help, a new surrounding appeared. This time it was a hospital. A young mother was lying in a bed, nursing her newborn. She looked happily into the crumpled little face, stroked the sparse hair on the almost bald head and cooed with tender, soft noises. The baby suckled with closed eyes seemingly unaffected.

The door opened, and a group of people in white coats entered. They seemed concerned.

The young mother looked up with happiness in her eyes.

Michaela screwed up her eyes. "But, isn't this ... Yes, it is ... One of my employees. How did she get here?"

"You don't even know her name?" the ghost inquired.

"Yes, yes, of course, I know it. It's Hoff. . . Hoffmann, uh no ... Benckhoff – yes, that's her name."

"What about her first name?" the ghost gently insisted.

"No idea." Michaela shook her head in anger. "I don't remember such things. It's not necessary to get the job done."

"Ramona," the ghost said. "Her name is Ramona."

Just this moment, one of the doctors in the blurred image started to speak. "Ms. Benckhoff, there's something you should know."

Ramona, a few years younger and appearing to be much more relaxed than these days, smiled at the doctors and nurses. She radiated the happiness of a young mother. "Yes?" She bent her head down to her child. "Isn't she sweet? Isn't she the sweetest thing you've ever seen?" She caressed the child's cheek.

"Yes indeed, she is," a different doctor confirmed, but her look did not share Ramona's happiness. "But ..."

Ramona looked up again. There was still no sign of

worry on her face, just interest. "Is there something else?"

"Yes." The doctor fell silent. "Unfortunately," he continued.

Ramona's expression changed. "What ... what is it? Is there something wrong with my baby? Or with me?"

"With your child," the doctor said.

Ramona glanced at the peacefully suckling baby. "But ... but everything's fine with her."

"Sadly, no," the doctor said. "There are certain kinds of birth defects that —"

"Birth defects? What birth defects?" Alarmed, Ramona stared at the infant at her breast who had just fallen into a peaceful slumber.

"It is a genetic disease," the doctor said. "We had to wait with that particular genetic test until after birth."

Ramona was quiet for a moment. It was apparent that she was trying to calm down. "So she has to go through treatment?"

The doctor looked at her and then exchanged glances with a nurse who seemed even more worried than he was. He then looked back at Ramona. He cleared his throat. "There is no treatment," he said.

"There is no treatment? What is that supposed to mean?" Ramona opened her eyes wide, the fear gleaming in them. "So it's not that bad that it needs to be treated?" She was shaking, despite the hope she was trying to put into her voice.

"It is ... bad." The doctor hesitated. "And it will get worse. Children with this disease rarely survive the first few months."

Ramona's face froze in that expression of hope and fear she had presented to the doctor. "A ... few ... months?"

she stammered in disbelief after seemingly endless minutes. She looked down at her peacefully slumbering baby. "But ... but ... I can't see anything. She looks completely healthy."

"It doesn't show – in the beginning," the doctor said. "But the genetic test is definitive. I'm so sorry."

Ramona watched her daughter full of desperation – and hope, against all reason. "It simply can't be," she said firmly. "She'll get over it. I know she will."

The doctor moved closer and put a hand on her shoulder. "I know, it's difficult to accept," he said, "but you have to. There is no cure. Make the most of what you have. Spend as much time as possible with your daughter. Unfortunately, that's all I can tell you."

The group dressed in white left the hospital room. When the door closed behind the last of them, Ramona hugged the small bundle in her arms. Tears welled in her eyes and streamed down her cheeks, silent tears, until finally a sob broke free.

"No," she whispered. "Oh god, no!" She hugged the child even closer, kissed and caressed it.

Michaela stood in silence. She appeared to be shocked. After a short while, she started to shake her head. "And I told her that her daughter would get better soon. I thought ... I thought she had a cold or something."

"No, she doesn't have a cold," the ghost said. He held up his flat hand and moved it in a circle, like he was wiping steam from a mirror.

As if by magic, the hospital vanished and a house appeared, the same one that was filled with laughter and brightly lit when Michaela had been a child.

Now, however, it was dark. The snow in the garden had sunk, as if it wanted to join the gloomy mood. There was a flickering light in one of the rooms on the first floor. They peeked through the window. Michaela did not think anymore about the fact they had to float in the air to be able to have this view. In a huge bed, an old man was lying, breathing with difficulty.

Michaela saw herself sitting in a chair next to her grandfather and continually glancing at him with a worried look. Finally her grandfather lifted a hand – hardly visible, but seemingly demanding a huge effort from him – and attempted to say something.

Michaela jumped up from her chair and leaned over him. "Don't, grandfather . . ." she said. "It's too much for you. Do you want something? Soup? Water?"

The old man slowly moved his head from side to side. Michaela sat down on the edge of his bed and took his hand. "Grandfather . . ." she whispered, and tears shimmered in her eyes.

"Not . . . bad . . ." her grandfather whispered. He swallowed hard, collected his strength, then continued. "Forgive me."

"Forgive you?" Michaela smiled under tears. "Why should I forgive you?"

"Because I –" Her grandfather had to stop and spoke again after a short break. "Because I'm leaving the company to him, not you. He is my son after all, my rightful heir," he said with a weak voice. "I can't do that to him. You have to keep an eye on him, though."

"How can I?" Michaela asked with tears in her eyes. "Once he owns the company, he can do whatever he wants."

Her grandfather tried to chuckle. "I was a good-for-nothing myself when I was young. When I took over the company, I changed. Once you have the responsibility ..." His voice became weaker. "Just take care of him," he whispered. "Watch him. Don't let him lose the company. It has to stay in the family. Promise me."

Michaela stared at him, overwhelmed by sorrow. "Grandfather ... grandfather ..."

"Promise me that," he demanded faintly.

"I promise," Michaela whispered almost imperceptibly. Exhausted, she rested her head in her hands and looked up again after a brief moment. "Grandfather!" A scream escaped her throat. "Grandfather!" A second scream, changing into sobs – into unrestrained sobbing. She threw herself onto the bed over her dead grandfather.

The scene was fading, but the sound of Michaela's sobbing and whimpering were heard until there was nothing to see. "Grandfather ... don't leave me alone ..."

Michaela swallowed hard. "That's enough," she said with a shaky voice. "Take me home, Ghost. I don't want to see anything else."

The ghost shook his head. "You have forgotten so much –"

"I haven't forgotten anything!" Michaela turned her head towards him, anger clear in her face. "Do you really believe I could've forgotten this? My grandfather's death? My grandfather? He was my life. He gave me everything he could."

"Except the company," the ghost said.

"Yes, yes. Rub it in deeper, the thorn in my flesh! You enjoy tormenting me, don't you?" She stared at him furiously.

"That's not why I'm here," the ghost said, unruffled. "But, you don't have to endure it much longer. We'll now get to the most important part."

"Oh no!" Michaela groaned and covered her face with

her hands. "You just can't stop, can you? Yes, I know I've made mistakes, but . . . but I couldn't –"

"No, you couldn't," the ghost said. "But one thing is still missing. You need to watch one more thing."

No sooner had he announced this, then they were standing again in the offices of Wittling & Co. It almost looked like the last time, all the lights were on, and there was music and laughter. Still, something was different. During her grandfather's reign, there was joy and a festive spirit all around. Now everybody seemed to be slouching in his or her own corner, victims of alcohol. There was a buffet, but everybody seemed to have found nourishment from the many bottles that were scattered all around.

A group of questionable looking men stumbled into the office, evidently in much the same state as the employees.

"Hey, Wittling!" one of the man from that group yelled across the room. "Where are you?"

"I'm here!" Michaela's father laughed and waved with a bottle of champagne, motioning them to come near. "Just come on in. There's plenty more where this came from."

"Oops." One of the men burped when he reached Wittling. "Well, we're ready for something different now. You are our best friend, aren't you?" He draped an arm around Wittling's shoulders and exhaled into his face, though Michaela's father did not notice his alcohol-soaked breath.

"Yes, of course." Michaela's father grinned at him. "You can have what you want. What's mine is yours."

"So, how about it?" the man asked. "A little cash?"

"Sure, sure!" Michaela's father swayed into his office.

"Just come on in."

The men followed him. He tried a few numbers at the safe, but when he realized that he had forgotten the combination, he opened his desk drawer and pulled out a small piece of paper. With quite some effort, he finally managed to set the lock to the right combination and opened the safe. He reached in and took out a bundle of hundreds. "Here, take it. You can have it all." He reached in again and distributed the safe's contents to the men.

The men laughed, stuffed their pockets with the money and — after a last look at the now empty safe — they staggered out of the room.

They were leaving through the company's front entrance when they almost collided with Michaela. She stepped back in disgust when she smelled the men reeking of alcohol. She watched them retreat down the sidewalk before she entered the building.

She stopped for a moment; her face froze. "Father?"

There was no reply.

"Father?" She crossed the floor towards the office that had belonged to her grandfather. It was the heart of the company, and it now served as her father's office during his rare and brief visits there.

When she reached the office, apprehensive disbelief showed on her face. She turned and quickly glanced back at the company entrance through which the group of drunken men had disappeared.

With suspicion, she approached her father who was still standing in the middle of his office, swaying in front of the open safe. "Father, how much did you give them?" she asked.

Her father looked at her with bloodshot eyes.

She stepped closer, took him by the shoulders and started to shake him. "How much did you give them?" she yelled at him.

"Everything – all of it," he slurred. "All that was in there."

"A-A-All?" Michaela stuttered, stunned. "That was all the money for salaries, for invoices – all of our cash, the company's liquidity. How could you?"

While Michaela was still staring at her own terrified face, this scene, too, started to fade like a dream.

"He died soon thereafter, didn't he?" the ghost asked, and it almost sounded as if there were empathy in his voice.

"Yes." Michaela hissed through her teeth. "No surprise with his lifestyle. But not before ruining the company."

"You had a hard time trying to hold on to the company."

Michaela snorted. "It was practically impossible! Debt, unpaid bills, no cash. I had to fire almost all the employees, sell everything that was sellable, our house – my grandfather's house . . ." She trailed off.

"You could've declined your inheritance," the ghost said.

Michaela shook her head slowly. "I had promised my grandfather. There was no way I could let him down." She set her shoulders. "Well, I did what I had to do. I saved as much as I could, kept the money together, turned every penny twice. That's how I managed."

"And saving became second nature, right?" the ghost asked.

"So what?" Michaela had apparently recovered from her shock. "There's nothing wrong with that, is there? Everyone ought to remember how important saving is.

That wouldn't hurt."

"It wouldn't?" The ghost asked nobody in particular.

"You have no idea what it means to lose your existence, to stand at the edge of ruin. You are just a ghost. You don't even exist."

"You really think so?" The ghost smiled.

Michaela turned around to answer the ghost, but he was gone, and she was back in her bedroom, feeling the cold floor under her feet.

"Brrr!" She crawled into her bed, pulling the covers up to her chin. "Well, I've never experienced anything like that before." She pulled the covers all the way up, over her ears. A great tiredness fell over her, and she was asleep before she could even think one more thought about what had happened.

≈⚏⚏≈

Bong, bong, bong, bong . . ."
This time Michaela woke up and knew it had rung twelve, without counting the tolls. She looked around. Nothing. No ghost.

Oh well, he had not mentioned a repeat visit. It must have been a one-time performance.

"And what about me?"

Michaela turned around quickly. She found herself face-to-face with a . . . face in the wall behind her bed, grinning cheekily at her.

"Don't you remember what she said? Others. Not just one – several."

"She? Uh . . . yes . . ." Michaela was overwhelmed. Was

all this really necessary?

The face peeled itself out of the wall and was completed by a round body. Everything about this creature was round. While the first figure had had no identifiable form, this one's was very distinct. It was about as wide as it was tall.

"The herald told you that you'll have several visits. There are three ghosts to be precise."

"Nobody told me about exactly what was coming," Michaela replied, sulking. "I would have braced myself."

"Well, now you know," snapped the little man. Again, Michaela could not recognize if this creature had a gender. But she preferred to think of it as a little man. Women were not this silly.

"So, what do you want?" Michaela asked and crossed her arms in front of her body. "Do you also have a few horror stories in stock? I'm getting used to it, you know."

"The Ghost of Christmas Past did mention that you were a hard nut," the grinning little man said. His face was moon shaped but, strangely enough, it was green. "But, the past is past. You had your chance."

"Yes, of course I did," Michaela said mockingly. "It's all my fault. I've been expecting something like this already."

"This year's Christmas is just a result of last year's Christmas," said the little man. "The present is based on the past."

"So you're the ghost of the present?" Michaela deduced from his remarks.

"The Ghost of Christmas Present," the little man corrected. "Christmas is our only territory."

"Thank god for that!" Michaela said. "I couldn't stand

having you around all year."

"You're a really bad little girl, you know that?" said the ghost.

"Hardly a girl anymore." Michaela laughed without sound. "I'm a grown woman!"

"That depends . . ." the little man answered. "It doesn't really matter. At least not to me. I'm just supposed to show you what this year's Christmas holds for you."

"What should it hold?" Michaela shrugged her shoulders. "The same as every Christmas for the past several years. It's a day like any other."

"If you believe that, you must be a very, very sad person," said the little man. For the first time he was serious.

"Not sadder than anybody else," Michaela said. "Life isn't fun. Ask your predecessor. What he showed me only confirmed it."

"Oh, it did?" said the little man. "Do you want more confirmation?"

Michaela shrugged again. "Do I have a choice?"

"Not really," the little man said. "I just wanted to be polite."

"Oh, how charming of you." Michaela offered a mocking bow.

"We strive not to cause too much excitement," the little man said.

"Not too much excitement?" Michaela laughed, this time a bit more sincere. "I haven't had this much excitement in years!"

"That's too bad," the little man said, "but it's nothing you can change now."

"What do you mean by that?" Michaela frowned.

"That's unimportant." The little man grabbed her

sleeve, and Michaela expected to start floating out the window, like last time. But nothing happened.

"Do you have to say *abracadabra* or something like that?" she asked, irritated.

"We also want to have fun," said the little man. He snapped his fingers, and the room in which they had just been standing was replaced by a street scene.

They were on a wide entrance ramp, and when Michaela looked around, she spotted a sign. 'General Hospital' it said.

"Uh, no. I don't want to go in there," Michaela said, repulsed.

"You know what to expect, don't you?" the little man asked.

"No, I don't," Michaela replied defiantly. "But a hospital – that can't mean anything good."

"Doesn't it remind you of something?"

"I've never been in a hospital," Michaela replied, as if the little man had asked her that.

"And yet it's not the first time you're here," the little man said. Another snap of his fingers changed the ramp into one of the long hospital corridors with countless doors to the left and right.

Michaela felt vaguely reminded of her dream, but everything looked completely different here. It had to be just a coincidence.

A woman was walking around, far away, in the background. They moved towards her, like on tracks, until Michaela could identify the person. "Ms. Benckhoff," she said, having paled.

Ramona walked up to one of the doors and opened it.

"No," Michaela whispered. "I don't want to see this."

"Are you not interested in the lives of your employees?" the Ghost of Christmas Present asked.

"Her private life is none of my business," Michaela said reluctantly.

"Then take a look at what's none of your business," said the ghost, and at once they were standing by the window inside the room Ramona had just entered.

Ramona was smiling and greeting the girl who was lying in a bed, attached to lots of tubes and machines. "How are you, sweetheart?" She leaned down and kissed the girl's hot forehead. "The doctor said you're doing a bit better."

"Yes, mommy, because you're here now." The girl beamed, despite the evident exhaustion that had overcome her. "I'm always fine when you're here."

Michaela saw how Ramona swallowed hard and looked to the window, directly into Michaela's eyes, which, of course, she could not see. When Ramona had composed herself, she turned back to her child. "I'm sorry I can't be here all the time. I have to work."

"I know, mommy." The girl seemed very understanding for her five years.

"The child ... is this old? But, the doctors had said —" Michaela trailed off. Ramona's eyes still burned in hers. Such shiny, pretty eyes. Although, they were probably just shiny from unshed tears. She had never noticed Ramona's eyes before, had hardly looked at the woman at all. They did not have to work a lot with each other.

"A mother's love overcomes a lot," the ghost said.

"Even death?" Michaela looked at the ghost, hopeful, almost begging. "Tell me the girl won't die. If she managed to get this far ..."

"I can only show you what's today," said the ghost. "My successor is responsible for tomorrow."

"Your successor?" Michaela frowned. "Oh right, you did say three."

"That's the way it is." The ghost fell silent.

A nurse entered the room. "Ms. Benckhoff, you should rest a while."

Ramona shook her head. "I can rest later," she said, "when everything's —" Again she turned her face to the window, and this time the glimmer in her eyes went through Michaela like lightning. Those eyes were so full of feeling, full of pain and suffering and so clearly without any hope.

Michaela had never seen such eyes, never before in her life. There was something in those eyes that she had always sought in the eyes of the women she met. But she had given up finding it. She had decided that what she was looking for did not exist, in any woman. And now —

"Even if you could get to a U.S. hospital, believe me, it wouldn't be of any use," the nurse said calmly. "It's too late."

"That's what I've been hearing since the first day!" Ramona jumped up agitated. "If only I could find the money somewhere . . ." She wrung her hands desperately.

"I'll get you something to eat," the nurse said. "You probably came here straight from the office."

Ramona looked at her. "Where else would I go?" she said with a weak voice. "My life is here."

The nurse nodded. "I'll get you a sandwich from the cafeteria. You need to eat something."

After a short while, the nurse returned. "This isn't necessarily what I would call a Christmas dinner," she apologized, "but our cafeteria is already closed. Everybody went home. The only thing left is sandwiches from the vending machine."

"That's fine," Ramona said. "It's nice that there are people who can just go home and celebrate Christmas. I'm happy for them. I wish I could, too. With Leonie." She glanced at the girl who had fallen asleep, but under the blanket they could see the labored breathing.

"I wish I could do more for you," the nurse said.

Ramona smiled. "You are doing more than your job requires. Everybody here is so nice to Leonie. I appreciate it very much."

The nurse sighed. She gently touched Ramona's shoulder, then left her alone with Leonie. She did not know about the other visitors.

"I can't believe there's nothing they can do for that child!" Michaela shouted indignantly. "That's not possible! With today's advances in medicine!"

"There's health care for the rich, and there's health care for the poor," said the ghost. "If even the rich can't be helped all the time with all their money, you know that the poor don't stand a chance."

"I wish . . ." Michaela stopped herself.

"What do you wish?" The ghost glanced sideways at her.

"Oh, nothing." Michaela fell silent.

Without warning, the scene changed again. This time, they were in a living room full of Christmas cheer and decorations. There was a tree in one corner, not as big as the one Michaela knew from her childhood but big enough to illuminate the whole room.

The table was crowded with plates. It was obvious it usually did not seat so many people. The table's extension was pulled out, but it still seemed too small for all the bowls, glasses, plates, shiny silverware, evergreen twigs and candles that were scattered across it.

"Come and eat, children!" Evelyn Majakowski balanced the giant goose as she carried it through a doorway that was nearly too narrow for it.

Suddenly people of all ages raced around her and into the room.

Two boys about ten years old, who looked like twins, hooted loudly and almost knocked her over. "Grandma, grandma, may we unwrap presents now?"

Evelyn Majakowski laughed; she was apparently used to such attacks. "Not yet. We're going to eat first."

"Oh, grandma, pleeeease!" The two begged with eyes hard to resist.

"Come on now; take your seats at the table." A man's voice, gentle but with authority sounded.

"You're just better at that than I am." Evelyn sighed.

"Well, you're the dear grandma after all. You don't have to be able to do that." Her son gave her a loving kiss on the cheek. "Okay, you rascals, it's enough now. Your mother and your grandma want to have some peace." He clapped his hands.

The two boys sat down, albeit very reluctantly.

A younger woman walked through the door with a dish full of steaming dumplings. "So, that's everything," she said. "Now we can eat." She set the dish onto the table.

"Without us?" Other voices came from the door.

Evelyn Majakowski jumped up with a beaming face. "Well, if you come to dinner late, you can expect that we already ate!"

"We got stuck in the snow," said a woman who looked like a young Evelyn Majakowski.

Behind her, a man of similar age entered the room. "If grandpa hadn't come and gotten us, we'd probably still be there."

"And you all made fun of me when I bought the car with all-wheel drive." Evelyn's husband came into the room. His face was red from the cold, and his eyes were gleaming.

"Where is Monika?" Evelyn Majakowski asked.

Her daughter shrugged her shoulders. "You know how teenagers are. She prefers to celebrate Christmas with her friends in a hut."

Evelyn Majakowski's face lost some of its joyful expression. "Too bad," she said. "I haven't seen her in so long. We could've finally all been together again. That's so rare."

"Merry Christmas, Grandma!" A cheerful voice from behind the door rang out, and a girl of about fourteen stepped out of the shadows.

"You are —" Evelyn Majakowski was speechless.

"I'd never do that to you, Grandma." The girl laughed. "I know just how much you love when we're all here for Christmas."

Evelyn wrapped her daughter and granddaughter in a hug. "That's right," she said. "And I hope that won't change any time soon."

The new arrivals hurried to get out of their jackets and defog their glasses. Evelyn and her husband took their seats at each end of the table, and the others filled in the chairs between them.

Evelyn raised her glass. "Merry Christmas to us all," she said and cast a proud glance around the table. "We have to be thankful that we can be together like this."

Everybody nodded and drank.

Evelyn didn't set her glass down. "We also want to remember those who are not as fortunate as we are. My co-worker, who has a very sick daughter — I invited her, but she didn't want to come. I thought it would do her good to get away from the hospital for a while, at least on Christmas Eve. But she said no. I think she's afraid that —" She stopped and looked gravely down at the table.

"She's afraid that her daughter would die and she wouldn't be there?" her husband asked gently. "I thought her condition had improved."

"It was just temporary. It seems it will be ... over soon," Evelyn said softly. "It is so sad. She is such a nice woman, a dedicated mother. The best person I know."

"I'd like to object to that!" Her son raised his glass and tried to cheer up the gloomy mood. "*You* are the best person I know. I'll drink to you."

"Thank you." Evelyn tried hard to smile. "You're right, we shouldn't lament on such an evening. But I'd like to make one more toast. To Michaela Wittling."

"Michaela Wittling? Are you insane?" her husband exclaimed. "She's a ruthless bitch."

"Oh, Georg, don't call her that." Evelyn waved her hand through the air. "She is not a ruthless bitch. She saved the company from ruin; she brought it up again and reinstated its good reputation — her grandfather's reputation. She is a woman to be respected. She could've just as easily walked away from it."

"Well, that wouldn't have been as much fun as torturing people and squeezing the last bit of life out of them, for outrageously little money," her daughter said.

"It's not always just about money," Evelyn protested.

"Really?" her daughter asked. "When did you last get a raise?"

"The company hasn't made a profit in years," Evelyn said. "It's not Michaela's fault. Her father ran it into the ground."

"I can see that you insist on making this toast," said her husband with a gentle smile. "Go ahead. Do what you have to do."

"She also has her good points," Evelyn insisted slightly annoyed. "She was such a happy little girl."

"Well, you wouldn't know today, now would you?" her son remarked. "All right. To Michaela – the queen of mean – Wittling." He raised his glass.

"You are impossible, Matthias," said his mother, but she smiled. "I won't drink to her like that. I drink to a terrific woman who just lost her way a bit. I would have liked to invite her to our Christmas celebration, so she could see how it is ... with a family and a Christmas tree. She doesn't even have one. I think that's sad."

"She won't show up suddenly at our door, will she?" Georg Majakowski asked suspiciously.

"No." Evelyn sighed. "Even if I had invited her, she probably wouldn't have heard me. She didn't even hear me wishing her Merry Christmas." She drank a sip and set her glass down. "And now, let's eat." As she looked encouragingly at her family, they saw her usual friendly face appear again. "On this special evening, we shouldn't worry about money. Let's just enjoy the time together. "

❧❦❧

ichaela turned around and wanted to ask the ghost a question when she realized that he had disappeared. At the same moment, a church bell began to strike. And with every strike a far-away figure rolled closer through the fog in which Michaela found herself now. She could see nothing but this figure. Her surroundings felt to her like a graveyard, a black hole that afforded only one view: the deeply veiled figure that came ever nearer.

"Seven," she counted. "Eight." She was afraid of the bell's last strike, since the apparition seemed determined to have reached her by then.

"Nine . . . ten . . ." Her voice quivered.

The figure's approach was slow and steady. It looked threatening in its dark cloak. Mute and silent, it grew bigger and bigger.

"Eleven . . . tw— twelve," Michaela counted.

With the last strike, the figure stopped in front of her. In contrast to the Ghost of Christmas Present, who a few moments earlier had left her without a word, this ghost was taller than she was. It was big and black, wrapped in something that looked like a coat or was maybe just a black nothing.

"Are you —" Michaela cleared her throat and tried to find her voice again. "Are you the successor, the ghost that follows the Ghost of Christmas Present?"

The figure said nothing.

"That's what you are, right?" Michaela looked over the black void in front of her. She felt like she could not see the top . . . or the head . . . or whatever it was. "We had the Ghost of Christmas Past, the Ghost of Christmas Present . . . and now, what's left? The future. The ghost who's supposed to show me the future. That has to be you."

Unlike its chatty predecessors, this ghost did not seem to have the power of speech but simply communicated through his appearance. The apparition seemed to wave with an invisible hand and started to move again, back the way it had come.

Michaela knew she had to follow and did not fight it. She suddenly felt like she was being carried on wings, as if the ghost's cloak was a flying carpet.

They arrived in the city, again not far from Michaela's company. There was a moving truck in front of the doors and a few people were watching strong men carrying out pieces of furniture, one by one.

"And she tried so hard," a woman said to a man standing next to her. "Wanted to save the family business. And now? All in vain. What good is a family business if you have no heirs?"

"Well." The man shrugged. "Should've brought a few children into the world. That would've been better for her. Maybe also would've made her happier. And they wouldn't have to scrape the name Wittling from the facade."

"She was not the motherly type," his neighbor replied. "But maybe she could have adopted some. There are so many children with no parents. And in the last years, the company was doing really well. She would have had the money. But no, she had to sit on it like a vulture."

"Now it's her carcass the vultures are feeding on!" said a man close to them and laughed. "Well, that's what you get for always only thinking about money, always about yourself, never about anything else."

"She could've done so much good with all that money," the woman sighed. "But now ... If they don't find any relatives, the money will go to the government. That's what she worked for so hard?"

"Each to his own," one of the movers said, putting down a table. "Up there, it looks like an office for the poorest of the poor. Looks like nothing has been replaced in a hundred years."

"Now, now, not that long!" A woman on the other side of the doors laughed. "But long enough. She even begrudged her employees a single pencil. They had to beg for every little thing."

"That's what can happen," the first woman sighed again. "I'm actually glad I don't have much. If you don't have anything you can't lose anything."

"You're right. It was all for nothing," a man who had not said anything yet agreed. "If you don't buy anything with your money, what's it good for?"

The woman laughed. "You're so right. Come on, let's go shopping!" Laughing cheerfully, they sauntered away.

Michaela stared at the ghost, waited for him to say something to her as the others had done. But he remained silent. The people on the street grew silent too. A green path appeared, Michaela recognized only after a while that it was the path to a grave.

The ghost led her wordlessly to a place where she could see the grave. A woman dressed in black stood in front of it. She seemed to be lost in silent communion. A few children played on a path farther away and were told to be quiet by a rough voice. Michaela could see only the back of the person standing at the grave before the figure turned to look at the children. Michaela saw the woman's profile.

"Ramona!" Michaela uttered.

It was an older Ramona, much older, but despite the grey hair, she was clearly recognizable.

When Ramona stepped to the side Michaela could read the inscription on the tombstone.

LEONIE

WITH YOUR SHORT LIFE YOU BROUGHT SUN INTO MINE

Ramona now carefully arranged a bouquet of flowers in a vase. "I have to go now, Leonie," she said. "Sleep tight. I'll see you tomorrow."

She turned and was about to step onto the path leading to the cemetery's gate when she stopped and went back to her daughter's grave. She took one flower from the vase. "I'll bring you new ones tomorrow." She smiled at Leonie's tombstone, which held an image of the little girl. "You won't miss just this one." She placed the flower on the grave next to her daughter's. "She was a good person. She just couldn't show it very well," she explained to her dead child.

When she turned to leave, Michaela could now read the inscription on the neighboring gravestone. It was her own name.

Michaela grabbed at the black cloak, tried to take hold, but she could not. The cloak had no real fabric, no substance at all. Michaela swayed. While watching Ramona walk away, she regained her composure.

"She is still a beautiful woman," she said. "I'm dead. She has to be old by now, but she's still beautiful. Why have I never noticed?" She gave her companion a questioning look, but he did not answer. Even though she no longer expected him to speak, she kept asking. "Is this how it's going to end? The child is going to die, I'm going to die, Ramona is going to be alone. None of us will be happy? Is that the future? Inevitable?"

The ghost's cloak fluttered slightly.

"But maybe it isn't the future after all? Maybe this is just a picture of what could be," she continued. "Is that it?" She looked back up into the blackness.

"You're not going to tell me, are you?" She shook her head. "It must not happen this way! I grow old and die, alone and lonely. Okay, that's the way of the world. But the child? That's no life to just be extinguished – just like that. She loves her daughter, and the child loves her. That's not fair. It must not be!" She struck out at the apparition, tried to hit it and only found her fists swinging freely through the air. "It must not happen! It must not happen!" she yelled. She hugged the tree at her side, kicked against it and kept screaming. "I don't want it to end this way! I just don't want it to! It must not . . . it has to . . . it has to . . . be different . . ."

Exhausted, she stopped. She was back in her bedroom and found herself fiercely hugging her bedpost.

"This . . . this . . ." She spun around herself. "This is my room. There is my bed! I'm back home!" She laughed. Once, twice . . . It was strange to laugh again. Suddenly she broke out in long laughter. She laughed almost hysterically, until the tears 'were streaming down her cheeks, until her eyes burned and her feet too – because she had kept spinning, like a top with her arms stretched wide.

"I'm not dead!" she yelled. "I'm not dead!"

She came abruptly to a halt.

"And if I'm not dead, then the other things haven't happened either. Then everything's still possible!"

She ran to the window and looked outside. It was still dark. The streets were brightly illuminated, but there were no people. It had to be the middle of the night.

She had no watch, she did not know what time it was, her inner clock was completely confused – and she did not care.

She dressed quickly, not noticing what she put on. She did not own much anyway that would cause a fashion disaster if worn together. She had barely slipped into her shoes, when she was already out on the street. She unlocked her car and drove to the office.

One of the clocks she saw on the way told her that it was four o'clock – much too early for anything, no matter what. But what day was it? She had spent nights in a different world, in many different worlds. Had it been as many days?

She took the street to the train station. She needed a newspaper, anything with a date, a weekday.

There was nobody at the newsstand yet. It did not open until five. Even the train station itself was still closed. But the papers that the newsstand was supposed to sell that morning were lying in front of the door. Michaela opened a packet and pulled out a paper. Christmas! It was December 25th! She was holding the special holiday edition!

She jumped around on the street as if bitten by a thousand fleas at once, danced and sang, "Christmas, Christmas! It's still Christmas!"

She hurried back to her car. When she arrived at the company, she was greeted by the deepest darkness. Of course. It was the same every day and especially on a holiday when her employees would stay at home. Usually, she went into her office and switched on her little desk lamp. She did not need more. Today she violated this rule, self-imposed for years. She entered the office and switched on the big lights.

Everywhere lights glared, but she soon came to realize that the explosion of light she had intended to set off was not going to happen. Some of the lights remained dark, a few others flickered briefly and then went out. The lights had not been used for too long, and apparently, Michaela had also neglected to have them maintained.

She did not let this dampen her good mood. She would have the lights fixed, would have everything fixed, until the office was ablaze like the sun itself.

First, though, she went into her office and picked up the receiver. The phone book – did she even have one? Most of the time she had Mrs. Majakowski connect her, if it was necessary.

"Well, who needs a phone book?" She remembered something she had heard the other day in passing. The number for directory assistance. It had changed since she had last used it – how long ago was that? . . .but Michaela had a good memory. She filed away everything, as insignificant as it might be. That had often given her an edge in her job, baffling her business partners.

She dialed the number. "Give me the General Hospital," she said to the voice who answered her call.

"Do you want me to connect you?"

"Oh . . . uh . . ." Obviously more had changed than just the number, since Michaela had last used directory assistance. "Yes, please," she said. "If that's possible."

"Of course. Just a moment. I'll put you through." Click. She heard the phone ringing on the other end of the line.

"General Hospital." It was a tired voice, so unlike the dynamic young one of the woman she had just talked to.

"Uh . . . I . . . Who is responsible for the sick children?"

"I beg your pardon. Is this some kind of prank call?" The voice on the phone sounded indignant.

"No, no, not at all," Michaela said quickly. "Only – you have a child there in the hospital who is very sick. Benckhoff, Leonie Benckhoff. I'd like to talk to the doctor who's responsible for her treatment."

"Oh, little Leonie, the poor thing. Such a sweet little

girl. And now —" The voice drowned in melancholy.

"Yes." Michaela's typical impatience returned. "Would you please connect me with the doctor?"

"He's not on duty," the woman said. "It's the middle of the night and Christmas."

"I know, I know." Michaela bit her lip. She had imagined this to be easier. Of course, there were not always doctors in the house, especially not during holidays. "Is there anything you can do? Couldn't you call him at home?"

"Now?" The woman was incredulous. "He'll be back in two days. You can talk to him then."

"In two days?" Michaela tried to control her anger. "It could be too late in two days. Leonie —"

"Leonie won't survive the holidays, the doctor said," the voice announced. She hesitated. "If it gets worse, I'm to call him, no matter what time — that's what he told me."

"And if she were to get better? I mean, if there was a chance —?"

"A chance? A chance for Leonie?" the woman asked, flabbergasted. "But . . . but she's much too sick —"

"That's why I want to talk to the doctor. Before it's too late." Michaela's urgent voice and the sympathy for Leonie finally broke the ice.

"All right," the woman said. "But you have to tell him this was your idea. That you insisted."

"Yes, yes, I will. Just hurry."

Michaela heard what sounded like the woman picking up the receiver on another phone and dialing. The tone for each number the woman pushed seemed to take an eternity, as if she were composing a complete symphony of touch-tones!

"Dr Kramer? ... Yes, I know what time it is. ... But, it's about Leonie." That apparently brought all the doctor's objections to a standstill. Michaela only heard how the woman said, "Yes, sir, all right." Then the voice returned from the distance back to her at the receiver. "He's coming," the woman said. "You'll be sorry if I find out you lied to me!"

"I didn't. I'm coming to the hospital," Michaela said. She ran out of her office. The lights stayed on.

❧ ✺ ✿ ❧

W hat on earth is happening here?"

Michaela heard the voice and smiled. She stood up and stepped out of her office into the corridor. "Ra– ... Ms. Benckhoff, it's just me."

"You, Ms. Wittling?" Ramona stared at her stunned. "But ... I thought ... burglars ... the light ..." she stammered. "I almost called the police."

"Good that you didn't," Michaela said with a smile. "Everything's okay. Except some of the ..." she pointed towards the ceiling, "lights."

"Yes, the lights ..." Ramona repeated and looked at the ceiling, too. "I didn't realize that we had any in here."

"Oh, by the way, you don't need to work this morning," Michaela said. "I believe you're needed at the hospital."

"At the hospital? Leonie ..." Ramona turned pale.

"No, no, nothing happened," Michaela reassured her. "I just thought you should be with your daughter. It's

Christmas."

"But ..." Ramona swallowed. "But I wanted to balance the books – so we wouldn't have to pay the fine again."

"If we get fined, then we'll just have to pay it," Michaela said. "I don't believe the Tax Office will mind. Just go."

"But ... but ..." Ramona stood motionless in the room, as if frozen in place.

"Ms. Benckhoff ..." Michaela stepped closer to her, grabbed her shoulders, spun her around and pushed her towards the door. "If you don't go right now, I'll drive you there myself." *Maybe I should anyway,* Michaela thought. It seemed like a brilliant idea to her. Holding Ramona's shoulders, she had suddenly felt a longing for that touch to never end. She quickly let go of Ramona. "Please, go. I'll manage by myself here."

Ramona turned around once more. "Ms. Wittling, is that really you? You are so different."

"I'm just like always," Michaela said and suppressed a grin. "You're just imagining things."

"If you say so ..." Confused, Ramona staggered away.

Michaela returned to her desk and waited. She did not work. She just waited for the call. "Wittling. Yes?"

As she had expected, Ramona's voice was at the other end of the line. "I ... it's me, Ramona Benckhoff ... I don't really know what to say, Ms. Wittling. I have to ..." She cleared her throat fiercely. "I have to ask you for some time off." Her voice became hectic. "I know, I should've requested it a few months in advance and ... and ... but even if you fire me ... Leonie ..."

"Just take as much time off as you need," Michaela said calmly, even though it took quite some effort because she would have preferred to jump to the ceiling for sheer joy. "What is the matter with your daughter?" She acted innocent. Ramona had to notice that in her voice, surely.

But she didn't. She was much too excited. She answered hastily, "Something has come up. They are doing clinical trials in the U.S. with children like Leonie, and it doesn't cost anything. Even the flight is paid for, the stay in the hotel . . . everything. It's like a miracle!"

"Yes, miracles happen sometimes," Michaela said. "Have a good flight." She hung up. She just could not control herself anymore. She had almost told Ramona the truth.

Slowly, she leaned back in her chair. She hoped everything would go well. The doctor said there was a fifty-fifty chance. That was not as much as she would have hoped for, but it was better than nothing. He would have to put Leonie into an artificial coma, so she would survive the flight to the U.S. for her treatment there.

At first, he had looked very skeptical when Michaela had come to the hospital. However, when she put the check on the table, when he read her name and realized she was not joking, his relief was written all over his face. "I would've done it myself," he said. "But I don't make much money as a doctor, and there are so many children who need help . . ."

"I understand," Michaela said. "But not all of them are going to die, if they don't get the proper care."

The doctor had nodded and squeezed her hands, visibly moved. "Even if it will give Leonie only a few more months, it's wonderful what you are doing. Ms. Benckhoff will be eternally grateful to you."

"I hope it will be more than a few months – as you have assured me before," Michaela said. "And on no account do I want Ms. Benckhoff to know about it. It is a clinical trial, everything's being paid for, and my name will not be mentioned. Have I made myself clear?"

"Not really," the doctor said. "But, if that's the way you want it —"

"I want it that way." Michaela got up and held out her hand to him. "You might as well get started. Ms. Benckhoff will be here soon. I'm going to let her know."

"But you don't want your name to be mentioned?" The doctor frowned confused.

"That's right," Michaela said.

Despite his confusion, the doctor respected her request.

Michaela looked around her office that now seemed lonesome and abandoned. It had never struck her just how shabby and run down it was. It was her grandfather's office, where in such a short time her father had caused so much destruction. In her grandfather's days, it was a proud office, not elegant or extravagant or modern, but solid and comfortable.

Her grandfather had loved English decor, so the desk was a monster — albeit a somewhat friendly monster — made of dark wood. There were the matching dark brown leather armchairs that served well during meetings. And the cabinets with tasteful carvings had always held a small assortment of different liquors for her grandfather's customers to sample, so they could experience the quality of the Wittling company's products for themselves — or drink to the closing of a good deal.

Her father had used all those supplies, and Michaela had never refilled them. If the customers wanted to drink something, then they should kindly buy it first.

She got up and ran her hand over the carved surface of the furniture. She did not need any ghost to remind her how much she had loved coming into this room while her grandfather was still alive. It radiated something that was hard to describe. Composure and calm, a natural generosity and strength and the confidence to take on the whole world from here. This was the haven from which everything took its leave and where everything returned; despite all the hard work, it had been full of laughter and fun. Humor had been one of her grandfather's most striking qualities. People loved him for it, and every other trait he had embodied. People could depend on her grandfather. He had never let anybody down.

Just one time his good nature outweighed his business sense: When he left the company to his son. For a moment, a dark shadow passed over Michaela's face, which, until now, had held a small smile. Then she sat down in one of the thick upholstered armchairs – realizing for the first time the cracks in the leather and the squeaking of the springs – and looked over to the desk where she had just been sitting a moment ago.

Now her grandfather was sitting there, writing with ink as he had always done. He was a modern thinker, but the atmosphere in his office was like a hundred years ago, and that was its appeal. The door opened and a little girl came storming in, ran towards her grandfather and laughed.

He immediately stopped writing, also laughed, opened his arms, caught the girl and lifted her up. When she was sitting on his lap, she looked over the table, as if she were in charge. "What does all that mean, grandfather?" the little one asked.

"You can't even read yet," her grandfather said. "I'll explain to you, when you go to school."

"Oh no, not until then? That's still soooo long to go! But I want to know now." She looked at him with begging eyes.

"Very well." Her grandfather leaned forward and began to explain the secrets of double-entry bookkeeping to her.

The girl listened attentively, as if she understood every word.

Michaela shook her head and smiled. *I was maybe five back then,* she thought. *Are all five-year-olds this way?* The image of another girl appeared in her mind. Leonie. She, too, was five years old. But fate had not been as kind as it was with Michaela at that age. *I hope everything goes well,* she thought again, and with a big sigh, she stood. What Ramona had wanted to do, she now had to do herself. Or should she go home?

No, she was not ready to give up each and every one of her habits. Nothing but two empty rooms were waiting for her at home. Should she buy a Christmas tree and invite Karina? That hardly would be the solution to the problem. If at all, she would have liked to invite Ramona – and Leonie. But, that could not be. They were on their way to America.

Well, work it was. That would be for the best. She left her office to retrieve the files from Ramona's desk.

It was a very tidy desk. The files were carefully stacked and sorted by keywords. Michaela looked through them and took what she needed. Just as she was turning to leave, she stopped for a moment, confused. What scent was that? The office smelled different. She stepped closer to Ramona's desk. The scent got stronger. She moved away and the scent vanished. It was ... Only when she had pushed Ramona out the door had she noticed this scent for the very first time. It was Ramona's scent.

Michaela inhaled deeply. Ramona. It would not keep for long, this scent, while Ramona was gone. Michaela turned around and sat down at Ramona's desk. She would work here, so she could save herself a few trips back and forth carrying the files.

That was, of course, the only reason.

❧❦❧❦

H appy New Year! Happy New Year!"
The employees returned to work and greeted each other cheerfully.

"Happy New Year, Mrs. Majakowski."

Evelyn Majakowski was dumbfounded and stopped in the doorway to Michaela's office. She had just wanted to drop off the mail. "H-Happy New Year, Ms. Wittling." She started to move again and put the envelopes on Michaela's desk.

All the time she kept staring in wonder at Michaela, who finally burst out laughing. "Yes, it's really me! How's your family? Survived the roasted goose?" She grinned.

"G-Goose?" Evelyn Majakowski could not escape stuttering. "Y-Yes, we did. It was really good."

"It looked like it would be."

Evelyn Majakowski looked at her as if she were seeing a ghost.

"Uh ... I mean I'm sure it looked it." Michaela remembered that Evelyn Majakowski did not know anything about her visit on Christmas Eve – and it would have been very difficult to explain. She got up. "Mrs. Majakowski, this year a lot of things are going to change around here. First of all, Ramona ... uh ... Ms. Benckhoff is in America on extended personal leave, so we'll need to find a replacement for her."

"She's ... in America?" Evelyn Majakowski was swaying.

"Take a seat," Michaela said and led her to one of the heavy leather chairs. She pointed at the cracks in the leather. "Those need refurbishing badly, including the springs. Could you please put that on the repair list?"

"Repair list?" Evelyn Majakowski stammered.

"Don't you have one? Then make one. A lot of the ceiling lights are burnt out, too."

"Yes, that's true," Evelyn Majakowski said. She tried to get a grip on herself. "The ceiling lights are on! That's why the office seemed so unfamiliar when I came in."

Michaela laughed. "That's probably what everyone thought! So, these things ... I assume you'll be taking care of them. Just find out what needs to be repaired and have it done. And then ... the desks – these are really not appropriate for work." She had noticed it when she had worked at Ramona's desk. "They're totally outdated, completely not ergonomic. Check the catalogues and see what the suppliers have that's current. Of course, some better chairs, too. I'm surprised everyone doesn't have bad backs by now!"

"Well, some have," Evelyn Majakowski said, still in shock.

"Then make sure those people get special chairs, even better ones than the others. And find out if you can arrange some time at a health resort for them."

"Ms. Wittling, I –" Evelyn Majakowski looked up at

her from her chair. "I just don't understand."

"Please call me Michaela," Michaela said. "You've known me from an early age, and you always used to call me that."

"Yes." Evelyn Majakowski got up. "Now I'm going to leave this office and then come back again. I must have gone through the wrong door."

"You haven't." Michaela grabbed her oldest employee by the shoulders and laughingly looked into her face. "And you're not dreaming either. Even if Christmas is over now, starting today, every day will be Christmas for me, the whole year. Everybody else should feel it, too. You remember how my grandfather ran the business. You're the only one here who remembers. Will you help me do it the same way? I'm not sure I can do it by myself."

Evelyn Majakowski nodded. "Yes, of course, I'd love to help you, but –"

"No buts!" Michaela interrupted her. "Go out and buy a coffee machine. For the whole office. One with all the bells and whistles. You know, one where you press a button and get any kind of coffee you want. I finally want to drink some good coffee again."

Evelyn Majakowski walked over to the door.

"Oh, and please call that children's charity. Those people who were here on Christmas. Let them know I have a big donation for them. You just go ahead and say how much – you know, the same amount my grandfather would've given."

"Yes." Evelyn Majakowski turned around again. "But I really think I'd like to double-check I'm in the right office."

"Go ahead." Michaela laughed. "And when you're done

with everything, come back here and we'll attack the rest."

The following month held one surprise after another for Michaela's employees. They hardly managed to overcome their collective shock at her new attitude. There were renovations, remodeling, refurbishing, re-painting – work conditions improved every day. At the end of the month when Michaela announced a raise for everybody, some said that work conditions had im-proved so dramatically they did not need a raise as well. Michaela understood they were joking; everybody could use a bit more money.

"Finally." Michaela leaned back in her chair and laced her fingers behind her head. Content, she looked around the room. Her office looked again the way she knew it did in her grandfather's times. The liquor shelves were well stocked, the leather chairs upholstered; everything was aglow with a new old shine.

There was a knock on the door, even though it stood open – as always now, since Christmas.

Michaela spun around in her chair. "Ramona!" She jumped up and cleared her throat. "Uh . . . Ms. Benck-hoff. You're back?"

"Yes." Ramona beamed and entered the room. She, too, had changed. "I hardly recognize a thing in here," she said and pointed behind her. "At first I thought I was in the wrong building."

"Now you see that you're not," Michaela said. She wanted to smile innocently, but it was hard for her. She wanted to pull Ramona into her arms. When she wasn't busy with work, she had been thinking of her every day for the past month. "We only renovated a bit."

"A bit?" Ramona laughed. "I believe Evelyn Majakowski is the only one who knew how it once looked here. The rest of us had only ever heard of the way it used to be."

"I'm sorry about that," Michaela said with a guilty look.

"I know, only by severely economizing could you get the company back in the black," Ramona said softly. "But it's nice that you're able to make these improvements now, and seem to enjoy it."

Michaela did not know where to look. Ramona's eyes were boring into her, like glowing coals burning through ice. She coughed slightly. "How is your daughter?"

Ramona beamed even more. "Leonie is healthy – well, as good as healthy. She still has to take it easy for a while, she still has to go through a few treatments, but she'll be able to start school this year, just like every other child. That . . ." She swallowed. "I never thought that would be possible."

"I'm happy for you," Michaela said. She remembered the headstone in the graveyard. "You wouldn't believe how happy," she emphasized, moved. She pointed towards the door. "Have you been to your office yet?"

Ramona stared at her. "My . . . office?"

"Yes, we had to move your desk for technical reasons." Michaela grinned. She tried to control herself and the grin that wanted to sneak to the corners of her mouth. "Has Mrs. Majakowski not shown it to you yet?"

"But I . . . I thought . . ." Ramona stammered, confused and let Michaela pull her towards her new office without showing any resistance.

Michaela grabbed the doorknob and swung the door open in front of Ramona. "Here it is," she said. "I hope you like the decor."

Ramona stood speechless at first then clasped her hands

to her mouth and walked into the room. She turned around to Michaela. "But . . . but this is . . ."

"The perfect office for the head bookkeeper," Michaela said with a smile.

"Head . . . head bookkeeper? But . . . but then it's not my office after all?"

"Of course, it is. Because that's what you are. Didn't you see? It says so on the door." Michaela pointed to the nameplate next to the doorframe.

Ramona stepped out and stared at the nameplate. There was her name and her title. Head of Bookkeeping.

"By the way, you've been paid at your higher salary level since January, as you might have noticed," Michaela said.

Ramona shook her head, still confused. "No. No, I hadn't noticed. I didn't need my own money in America. Everything was paid for. I haven't checked my bank account yet."

"Well, then go and check it now," Michaela said. "Your Christmas bonus should be there, too."

"Christmas bonus?" Ramona staggered over to the office chair she apparently now accepted as her own, even though it was clearly new, and sat down.

"I believe this may all be a bit much for you," Michaela said sympathetically. "The others have had a whole month to get used to it."

"A whole month . . . Just one month," Ramona said. "It seems to me more like ten years."

"Not that long!" Michaela laughed. "Maybe . . . uh . . ." She cleared her throat. "Maybe I could tell you more about it over lunch. Would you like to have lunch with me?"

Ramona gave her a blank stare. "Lunch? Me? With you?"

"Well, only if you'd want to," Michaela said. "Take it easy today. Just get used to everything first." She retreated, closing the door behind her. Uh-oh! That was taking it a bit too far. Ramona had been occupying her thoughts so much that she felt very close to her. But Ramona did not know that. How could she know?

"Ms. Wittling?" The door opened.

"Yes?" Michaela turned around in the corridor.

"I'd like to have lunch with you." Ramona smiled. "Very much."

"Well ... all right." Now Michaela was the one stammering. "One o'clock? Would that be okay?"

"Yes." Ramona kept smiling.

Michaela was absorbed by that smile, it penetrated her, filled her completely. She had to force herself away from it. "See you at one," she said and hurried back into her office.

"Mrs. Majakowski, come quickly!" Michaela stood in her office doorway and beckoned Evelyn Majakowski toward her.

Evelyn raised her eyebrows in surprise, but during the past month, she had gotten used to quite a bit. Michaela probably had another idea for renovation or improvement. She walked to Michaela, and they entered the office.

Contrary to her now usual habit, Michaela closed the door behind her. "You have to help me," she said — and appeared to be extremely nervous.

"I'd love to, any time, you know that," Evelyn said.

"It's ... it's —" Michaela stuttered and did not know where to put her hands.

"What's the matter, Michaela? What's wrong?" Evelyn

laughed, surprised. She had never seen her boss this in-
secure.

"I ... I – well, I haven't eaten out much in the last few
years. Too expensive and too time consuming,"
Michaela said. She paced excitedly around in her office.
"And now ..." She hesitated, unsure, so unlike herself.
"Can you recommend a nice restaurant?" she finally
blurted out.

"A restaurant?" Evelyn was surprised. "Around here?"

"Yes ... or ... actually, it doesn't matter where. It just
has to be nice."

"Nice?" Evelyn was even more surprised. "For what
occasion? Do you want to go out to dinner?"

"Uh ... no ... lunch," Michaela mumbled. It was
dawning on her that Evelyn would not just recommend
any restaurant without knowing the circumstances. She
should have consulted a restaurant guide.

"Lunch?" Evelyn asked. "I hear there are quite a few
cheap eats around here for lunch. I can go and ask some
of the staff where they always go. I cook at home in the
evening; I never go out for lunch."

"I'd rather –" *It would be better if none of her employees
were in the restaurant,* Michaela thought. But, if she would
tell Evelyn that, she would have to explain why. "It's
okay," she said. "Maybe Ms. Benckhoff knows where to
go."

"Ms. Benckhoff? I hardly think she'll know any restau-
rants. She used to spend every free minute with her
daughter at the hospital."

"Maybe she'll remember something, once we're on
our way," Michaela said.

"On your way? She's going, too?" Evelyn gave Michaela
a blank stare.

"Uh ... well, I thought ... I mean, she just returned today, her daughter is doing better, and we haven't celebrated her promotion yet either ... so I thought —" Michaela talked herself into a tangled chaos. She suddenly stopped, jerked around, sat down behind her desk and opened a file. "I just thought that deserved taking her to lunch," she finished angrily.

"I could organize a small company party," Evelyn suggested. "Then everybody could join." Michaela seemed so intent on that recently.

Michaela closed her eyes for a moment. She had to collect herself. What had she been thinking, asking Mrs. Majakowski for help? "Yes, all right, a little party ... We can do that," she agreed. "There are enough reasons, what with all the changes."

"I should think so," Evelyn said. She studied Michaela thoroughly. "There is a small restaurant," she started carefully after a while. "My husband and I used to go there all the time. I don't really know if it's still there. But it always was very nice."

"Really?" Michaela looked up.

I was right, Evelyn Majakowski thought. *I didn't get it wrong. There is something else.* She smiled. "My husband proposed to me there for a second time," she said. "Before our silver wedding anniversary. It was very romantic."

"Uh ... It doesn't have to be romantic," Michaela said with unease.

I think it does, Evelyn thought. "Well, keep thinking about it," she remarked casually. "I'll go and get the address for you. Do you want me to make a reservation for you?"

Michaela cleared her throat. "Yes. Yes, please," she

said and did not dare lift her eyes off the file anymore. "For one o'clock, two people."

Evelyn Majakowski nodded and left the office smirking.

∞⊱⊰∞

I'm overwhelmed from all the new developments," Ramona said. "I can hardly believe it. It's so ..." She smiled at Michaela who was sitting opposite her at the small table in the restaurant. "It's all so unexpected."

Michaela looked into those eyes that seemed so familiar to her and so incredibly beautiful. She wanted to see more of these eyes ... wanted to see them closer. She cleared her throat fiercely and pushed her food around her plate. "As I said before, the others were able to get used to it over time. You will, too."

Ramona laughed lightly. "I'm not so sure about that. It's like a dream – and I think any minute now I'll wake up and everything will be over." She leaned forward, and Michaela noticed the scent that had attracted her attention at Ramona's desk. She swallowed hard. Ramona continued, "Just to think that Leonie is cured now, that she'll be able to come home – that's like a miracle. That would have been more than enough for me. But now this ... Everything you've done –"

"I haven't done anything," Michaela said. "That was all long overdue."

Ramona smirked. "I agree. It was. But I never would've thought that you –"

"That I would develop into a normal human being?" Michaela continued.

"No, that's not what I wanted to say." Ramona seemed startled. As if Michaela would revert back to her old self and fire her for such a remark.

"Yes, you did," Michaela said. She smiled at Ramona. "And you would've been right. I was —" She put her fork down and laced her fingers under her chin. "I was so busy pulling the company out of the depths that I missed the point when I felt dry land under my feet again. I thought you had to choose only one: either be generous — which for me meant being wasteful — or save every dime and spend only when absolutely necessary to make sure the company would never be at risk." She sighed. "It was a big mistake. I can only hope you'll forgive me."

"I . . . Forgive you?" Ramona stared at her. "How did you get the idea I need to forgive you?"

"I . . ." Michaela grabbed her fork again and started rearranging her food, so she would not have to look at Ramona. "I would like it if you did. I certainly didn't make your job easy."

"If anything, that applies to all your employees, not just me," Ramona replied. "You should invite them all out to lunch."

"Mrs. Majakowski suggested something like that, too." Michaela sighed. "That idea seems to be catching."

Ramona laughed. "It's just a suggestion," she said. "Nobody expects that of you after everything you've done. All morning I've been hearing nothing but Ms. Wittling this and Ms. Wittling that. How you turned everything upside down and how happy everybody is about it."

"I rather think I put things back the way they were,"

Michaela said with a smile. "My grandfather ran the company this way, and now I'll continue in his spirit. All that in between ... that was ... My grandfather wouldn't have wanted that." Ashamed, she looked down at the tablecloth.

"But you're not your grandfather!" Ramona said resolutely. "You're selling yourself short. How many people would've managed to do what you've done? Don't forget: I'm the bookkeeper; I know the numbers. Also the numbers you had to start with."

"You needed a lot of red ink back then," Michaela said.

"Yes." Ramona leaned her elbows on the table and studied Michaela. "I didn't have much time to think about other people the last few years," she said. "But you always were a role model for me. I thought, if you can fight, I could, too. Every time Leonie ..." She swallowed. "Every time she was getting worse, I thought about the energy you emanated, of this never wavering conviction that you can do everything if you just work hard enough. You showed me that. And I'm very thankful for it."

Michaela looked at her puzzled. "You saw something positive in that?"

"Yes. Because, you see, most people are different. They give in to their fate, they lament, they blame others, give up ... don't do anything anymore. But not you. You always fought. You never let it get you down. That is admirable."

Michaela swallowed. "*You* are admirable," she said after a while. "What you did for your daughter ..."

"I did what every mother would do for her daughter," Ramona corrected. "No mother would give up on her child. Every mother would grab the last straw if it could save the life of her child. But you don't have any children. You —" Ramona interrupted herself. "Oh, I'm sorry," she said. "I didn't want to offend you. That's none of my business."

"That I don't have any children?" Michaela shook her head slightly. "Well, that's a fact. You're not offending me by stating it."

"Have you never ..." Ramona hesitated. "Have you never wanted any?"

Michaela thought about it for a moment. "No, I don't think so," she said after a moment. "To be honest, I never really thought about it."

Ramona laughed softly. "I can't understand that. I've always wanted children. I'd love to have a whole house full. That was always my biggest wish."

"Now I'm deeply disappointed that bookkeeping wasn't your biggest wish," Michaela said, and when Ramona raised her head startled, she looked into mischievous eyes.

"You're not serious," she said relieved though still a bit uncertain.

Michaela grinned. "No, I'm not. Even though I personally never wanted to have children, I believe that children are our future. And it's a shame how this future is neglected these days."

"Yes, the dreadful state of education and all that." Ramona sighed. "If I could afford a private school, I would not want to subject Leonie to the public school system, considering how poor it is."

"You —" Michaela stopped herself. "Where is Leonie's father?" she asked. "Isn't this something that concerns both parents, not just the mother?"

Ramona's face closed up. "Leonie doesn't have a father," she said.

"He's not living with you, you mean?" Michaela was slightly confused.

"No, he's not living with us," Ramona confirmed stiffly.

"I'm sorry." Michaela looked at her. "Did I step in it now? Or —" Her look changed to one of concern. "Is he no longer with us?"

"Even if that were the case, I wouldn't know about it. I don't even know his name," Ramona said.

"Oh." Michaela did not know what to say now. She did not expect that of Ramona.

Ramona sighed. "Before you now crown me queen of the one-night stands: It was artificial insemination."

That surprised Michaela even more. Ramona did not exactly look like she would have to resort to that. Surely, any man would have volunteered to help her have a child the natural way.

"I wouldn't have wanted it any other way," Ramona said, as if she wanted to close the subject.

But Michaela's curiosity was aroused. "Were there health problems?" she asked. "I mean, that you couldn't . . . the normal way?"

"Normal. What's normal?" Ramona said. "Apparently I'm not." She took a deep breath. "At least not for a lot of people."

"I . . . Ramona, I'm sorry . . . But I don't understand." Michaela had switched to Ramona's first name because the conversation suddenly seemed much too intimate for last names.

"I'm a lesbian," Ramona said. "I don't have sex with men."

Michaela was stunned, but her heart jumped up and

down in her chest. Her throat was tight. Even though she had felt so attracted to Ramona, she had assumed . . . After all, Ramona had a child.

"I hope that's not grounds for dismissal," Ramona said in that moment. "I was just getting used to the new office."

Michaela tried to get rid of the lump in her throat, but the clearing turned into a cough. "Not grounds, no," she said with some effort.

"Or maybe you'd like to revoke my promotion?" Ramona asked. "Now that you know more about me?"

Michaela violently shook her head. She still had trouble speaking. "No. No way. You are the best person for the job."

"I hope my revelation won't be a burden on our relationship in the future," Ramona said. "I've had quite a few bad experiences in the past."

"Our . . . relationship," Michaela replied with difficulty, after she had calmed down a bit, "has nothing to do with this." *Or does it,* she thought. "It's only your work that counts."

"I'm glad," Ramona said. "I'd prefer it that way."

"Well . . . well, then we agree."

Michaela did not know what to do with that answer. Did this mean Ramona did not want any private contact with her at all, only professional contact? On the other hand – she had not offered her any private contact yet. That was still just in her head – a pipe dream.

They returned to the city center, parked the car and just before they reached the office building, Ramona stopped at a shop window. "I'd like to get some flowers – for my new office," she said. She nodded at Michaela. "You just go ahead, I won't be long."

Michaela looked at the flower bouquets in the window, not tempted by any of them. "We're walking back together," she replied. "But you should go in there by yourself. Flowers really aren't my thing. I'll wait outside."

Ramona looked at her slightly puzzled but then entered the store and focused on picking a bouquet, as Michaela watched her from outside through the window.

"Mike? You're out shopping?"

An all too familiar voice made Michaela turn around.

"That's something new," Karina said and smiled at her.

"I'm ... I'm not shopping. I'm just waiting," Michaela replied uncomfortably. The last time she had seen Karina she had been some kind of angel. She thought it rather strange to suddenly be faced with the real woman, standing opposite her in the flesh.

"You're waiting? Who are you waiting for?" Karina craned her neck and tried to recognize the person in the store.

"And that would be any of your business?" Michaela asked. Her new self did not fit with Karina. She lapsed back into her old habits, quickly becoming rude and defensive.

"No, but I'm curious. You should know that about me, at least." Karina flashed her a smile.

"We haven't seen each other in a while." After her supernatural encounter with Karina's apparition, Michaela felt she knew Karina even less than before.

"That's true. Well, why don't we get together soon and —"

At that moment, Ramona stepped out of the store, a bouquet under one arm and a potted plant in the other.

"All right, we can go now," she said to Michaela.

Karina cast a highly interested glance at Ramona and examined her intently before finally finishing her sentence. " – or maybe not," she said. It was obvious she had made the decision in that moment. She smiled at Michaela. "I presume we won't be seeing each other any time soon," she remarked smugly. "Ciao, Mike, my lady love. And have a good time!" She laughed and continued on her way, giving a small wave.

Ramona stared at her retreating back with surprise. "An acquaintance of yours?"

"Yes." Michaela coughed. "An acquaintance." She took the potted plant from Ramona. "May I?"

"Thank you. I'll carry the flowers." Ramona held on to the bouquet, and they walked back. "Mike?" Ramona asked after a short, contemplative pause. "Did I hear correctly?"

"A short version of my name. Only ..." Michaela coughed again. "Only a few people call me that."

"A bit unusual," Ramona pondered. "I mean, I know Micha or Ela, but Mike ... that's more a name for ..." She trailed off but gave Michaela a sideways glance with a knowing smile.

"Yes," Michaela said. "That's more a name for ..." She too did not finish the sentence.

"And you let me go on stammering like that?" Ramona remarked slightly accusatory.

"It was –" Michaela swallowed. "It was a surprise for me," she defended herself.

Ramona kept smiling. "For me, too. In a certain way," she said. "Well, I mean, I haven't thought much about those kinds of things in the past few years."

"You had other things on your mind," Michaela nodded. She held the door open for Ramona. "That's why I can only repeat what you said earlier: I hope it won't be a burden on our professional relationship."

&

ichaela came home and dropped exhaustedly into a chair. Unlike the offices, her apartment still looked exactly as it did before Christmas. Nothing had changed. She simply had not had time for it. The ghosts could say what they wanted, but business was just more important.

Meanwhile another month had passed. There was still snow on the ground, but the crocuses were sprouting and announcing the imminent arrival of spring. Michaela coughed. For a few days now, she had been struggling with a cold that did not want to go away. Evelyn Majakowski had recommended she stay home, Ramona too, but Michaela did not want to hear any of it. She had not been sick for years, why should she suddenly be? Now, when life was light and friendly?

Since their lunch together Ramona and she had not had a private conversation, apart from Michaela asking about Leonie's health. Ramona had placed her full attention on getting settled into her new position as head of bookkeeping, and whenever they needed to talk, it was about business – bookkeeping files, payables and receivables, cost centers. Those were the words Michaela kept hearing come from Ramona's lips.

Still, she was always glad for a chance to watch her mouth, when Ramona came into her office and smiled at her, even for pure business purposes. There was a quiet agreement between them not to talk about what they had revealed to each other. And, even though Michaela would at the very least have loved to go to lunch with Ramona every day, she had not suggested it again.

Great, Michaela thought. *Now we both know we're gay and stay away from each other because of it. We'd probably spend more time together if we had continued assuming we were straight.* She sighed. *Life is playing cruel games with us.*

She felt a hot wave racing through her head. She had a fever. She had kept herself medicated all day, but the pills seemed to be losing their effect now. She lifted herself out of the chair with a groan. She would have to pop another pill.

The doorbell buzzed. Michaela ignored it. Probably just a door-to-door sales rep peddling magazine subscriptions. She had no head for that today.

It buzzed again.

Michaela was halfway to the bathroom to get the pills and gave a big sigh, wishing she could just turn off the doorbell. She hoped whoever was standing in front of her door would soon give up.

"Ms. Wittling?"

Michaela felt faint. Was she starting to hear voices now?

"Ms. Wittling? It's me, Ramona Benckhoff."

Ramona. Ramona? Michaela jerked around, startled, and almost fell to the floor, weak as she was. She pushed herself from the wall with some effort, staggered to the door and opened it. "Ms. Benckhoff?" she asked softly. "What are you doing here?"

"My god, what's wrong with you?" Ramona answered Michaela's question with a question. "You look even worse than you did at the office just a while ago."

"I was just about to take some medicine," Michaela croaked. Her voice was failing. Everything seemed to hurt.

"You just don't know how to take care of yourself!" Ramona scolded her, seized her arm, supported her and led her back into the living room.

Michaela dropped into the chair she had just left.

"This is your apartment?" Ramona asked horrified. She looked around astonished.

"Yes. I . . . I haven't had a chance yet –"

"Don't talk." Ramona interrupted her. "It must hurt."

Michaela nodded, her face a pained grimace.

"I assumed something like that when I saw you earlier today in the office," Ramona said. "I bet you have the flu."

"Cold," Michaela mumbled.

"No, it's not just a cold. Believe me. I know better. I've spent a lot of hours in the hospital. You have to stay in bed and rest. This will take a few days."

Michaela opened her eyes wide.

"Yes," Ramona said. "That's what you get for neglecting your health for too long. You should've listened to Mrs. Majakowski and me sooner." She looked around, left the room. There was silence, then Ramona returned. "My god, your bedroom is a fridge. How can you sleep in that cold?"

Michaela wanted to say something but could not because her throat was on fire and felt like it would be swollen shut at any moment.

"Let's turn up the heat. You shouldn't go in there until the air is warmer," Ramona decided.

"No . . . heat," Michaela whispered, hoarse and soundless.

"No heat? You don't have heat in your bedroom?" Ramona shook her head. "And here I was thinking I had no luxury at home." She looked skeptically at the couch that must have seen better days before Michaela was even born. "I'll go get the blankets," she said. "We can warm you up at least. And then I'll make you some tea."

Michaela pointed at her throat and gestured as if she wanted to wring it.

"Your throat is swollen, right?" Ramona said. "Don't worry. We'll get you more comfortable." She turned around. "If I'd known how you were living, I would have made some soup for you and brought it with me," she said. She turned back to Michaela. "Will I survive the shock of seeing the kitchen?"

Michaela frowned and looked guilty.

"Oh my," Ramona sighed. "I guess I'll have to run to the store first. Your keys?"

Michaela pointed at the table.

"I see." Ramona took the keys. Then she got the blankets, covered Michaela with them and left the apartment.

When she returned, Michaela was breathing noisily from the chair, and her cheeks were glowing. She had her eyes closed but was not sleeping.

"I was also at the pharmacy," Ramona said and held up a small bag. "Since you can't swallow, I got you suppositories for your fever."

This catapulted Michaela back among the living, despite her condition. She stared at Ramona, her eyes wide open.

Ramona laughed. "You can do it yourself. I'll put them in the bathroom." She vanished for a moment and then returned. "Come on, I'll help you." She grabbed Michaela under both arms and pulled her out of the chair. "Lean on me. I won't collapse," she told her.

Michaela did not really have a choice. With Ramona's help, she dragged herself into the bathroom.

Ramona left her and disappeared into the kitchen.

A short time later, she heard Michaela leaving the bathroom. She hurried into the hallway and supported her again. "The soup and the tea will be ready in a moment. I'm also boiling some chamomile. The steam will help you swallow and breathe again."

Michaela did not believe she would ever be able to do that again, but her whole body ached so much it made her forget this doubt. Ramona helped her lie down on the couch and covered her with the blankets. "You should sleep," she said gently. "Your body can fight the virus faster if you do." She tenderly touched Michaela's forehead. "You feel like an oven." A concerned look swept over her face – and something else.

That look was the last thing Michaela saw before she fell into a fitful sleep. The medicine had started to work.

❧ ⸙ ❧

When she awoke, it was daylight. An early bird was chirping outside her window – one of those who would risk freezing to death while building a nest for his companion who would make the journey north later in the spring.

She tried to sit up. Her head hurt. She sighed. There was movement in the chair next to the couch.

"Are you awake?" Ramona's head, hair rumpled, was nestled between her own and Michaela's coat. There had been no blanket left for her. She got up and stretched. "Maybe you would like to try some soup now."

Michaela stared at her. "You —" She had no command over her voice, it felt frozen, despite the heat she still felt radiating from her body. "You've been here all night?" she croaked so quietly that Ramona had to read it off her lips.

"Yes, I . . . It was easier this way," Ramona said.

"Leonie," Michaela whispered.

"She's staying with Mrs. Majakowski. I had intended to pick her up last night, but Mrs. Majakowski said it was no problem having Leonie stay over. They have a spare bedroom."

Michaela sank back onto the couch. She could not believe that Ramona had stayed the night — and that she had no memory of it.

Ramona went into the kitchen, and Michaela could hear her moving around. That had never happened before. A woman in her kitchen, which she herself never used. A woman in her apartment was a rarity by itself, but in the kitchen — that was a first. No woman had ever been in her kitchen alone, much less cooking in there.

It did not take long for Ramona to return with the soup. "I just warmed it up a bit," she said. "I made it last night." She also brought a shelf from the kitchen. She must have taken it down, an easy thing since the kitchen was nearly bare. She placed it across Michaela's lap like a tray and put the soup bowl on it. "There we go — and just a moment," she said like a good nurse, pulling the blanket around Michaela and propping a pillow behind her back.

Michaela tried to say something, but nothing came out.

"Go on. Eat. Your voice will come back soon enough,"

Ramona said with confidence. "The warm soup will help."

Michaela obediently spooned up the soup and was surprised that she was indeed able to swallow, albeit with significant effort and pain. She felt better with every spoonful she managed to swallow. She could not say if the soup was good; her taste buds were unable to discern anything. When she cleared her throat after a while, it was with sound. "Thank you," she whispered.

"You're welcome," Ramona said.

Her smile was so charming, so sweet that Michaela felt not just hot from the soup and the fever. "You better go home now," Michaela croaked hoarsely.

"During work hours?" Ramona grinned. "It's a regular weekday."

"Oh, right," Michaela whispered. "I had completely forgotten."

"That you could ever forget something like that . . . I'm still not used to that." Ramona smiled and took the soup bowl from Michaela. "Would you like more?"

Michaela shook her head.

"I'll get you a big pot of tea now. You have to drink a lot. Then I'll go. I'll be back later to check on you. Do you want me to get something else for you? Would you like to eat anything special?"

Michaela shook her head. "No, thank you," she whispered. "I have no appetite."

"That doesn't matter," Ramona said. "You have to eat. I'll think of something."

After she set Michaela up with everything she would need, she took her things and said good-bye. "I'm really worried you have no phone here in your apartment," she said with a frown. "I hope nothing's going to happen. I'll be back as soon as I can."

"I'm all right," Michaela said. "You don't have to come back."

"That's not up for discussion," Ramona said with a smile. "I'll be back, no matter what."

Michaela looked at her and wished she did not have to go at all. "If there's something at work I have to take care of, could you please bring it with you?" she said.

"I will do no such thing." Ramona laughed. "You are sick. You have to rest. You'll have to do without work for a few days. As hard as that may be for you." Once more she checked the pillow behind Michaela's back, the level of tea in the pot and the amount of tissues and pills. "See you later," she said and seemed to hesitate.

"See you later," Michaela said.

When the door shut behind Ramona, Michaela felt as if the sky had darkened, as if part of her life had gone out the door. But, she was so exhausted that she fell asleep a few minutes later.

She awoke from an unexpected noise. It seemed to come from inside her apartment. There was groaning and moaning, mixed with a few other, nondescript sounds. She listened hard to identify the noise, but she could not. Some kind of ghosts again? In the middle of the day?

Cautiously, she got up and stepped into her slippers. All of her bones hurt, but that did not stop her from tip-toeing into the hallway. The noise came from her bed-room. Slowly she made her way to the door and peeked around the corner.

She could not believe her eyes.

Mrs. Majakowski was leaning over some kind of metal box, and Ramona was crawling around on the floor behind it, on all fours.

"Just a moment, I think I've got it now," she said to Mrs. Majakowski.

The box crackled and a red light glowed behind Evelyn Majakowski. She turned around. "Ah, there you are, Michaela," she said. "I'm so glad you're doing better. Ms. Benckhoff told me horror stories about yesterday. That must have been just terrible."

"Yes," Michaela said, still completely confused. "What . . . What is that?"

"A heater." Evelyn Majakowski stepped aside, and Ramona stood up. "A propane heater. We had it in the cellar, from camping. We don't use it anymore. We used to go camping all the time, but now that my husband and I are older, it's too much trouble for us. When Ramona told me you have no heat in your bedroom . . . To get better you need warmth. You can't lie in a cold room."

"And so the two of you hauled that thing all the way up here?" Michaela stared at the oddly shaped heater, which now held a burning flame.

"It wasn't really that heavy," Ramona said. "The propane tank was the heaviest part."

Michaela looked at the heater. It almost seemed to be a real little fireplace. A big glass door in the front let the fire appear very realistic.

"Well, I'm off now," Evelyn Majakowski said. "You'll be staying for a while?" she asked Ramona.

Ramona nodded.

"Do you want to leave Leonie with me tonight again?" Evelyn asked. "I like her being around. It's so nice having a child in the house again. Mine were young so long ago, and my grandchildren don't come around very often."

"Leonie is mad about you." Ramona smiled. "She loves

your cookies." She looked around the room. "I'll come by later. If Ms. Wittling isn't feeling worse." She gave Michaela a worried look.

"By the way, who's at the office?" Michaela asked.

"There's not much going on," Evelyn Majakowski said. "We'll manage by ourselves. Don't you worry." She smiled mischievously. "I know, you can't image it, but everything's running smoothly without you."

"And now, back to bed!" Ramona ordered. "You've been standing there for too long already. You're feet must be freezing!"

Michaela felt too weak to resist the combined force of these two women. Ramona got the blankets from the living room. Michaela lay down, and Ramona tucked her in like a child. "Tomorrow, I'm going back to the office," Michaela grumbled.

"Hardly!" Ramona and Evelyn laughed.

After Evelyn had left, Ramona set a mobile phone on Michaela's nightstand. "You'll find the expense in the next report," she said. "As head of bookkeeping, I took the liberty of buying a company mobile phone. Now you can call if you need or want something. I programmed in the number of the office. Just push the 1 and then the green button."

"A company mobile phone?" Michaela was flabbergasted.

"If you want, you can also pay for it yourself – or I will. I just wanted you to be in reach. To think you don't have a phone here . . ." She shook her head in disapproval.

Michaela felt weak and noticed that she was exhausted and started to nod off. "Thank you . . ." she said softly and closed her eyes. She wanted to keep looking at Ramona, but could not. She fell asleep.

❧❦❧❦❧

One week later Michaela had recuperated enough that she was gripped by an inner restlessness she could not contain. She got dressed and drove to work.

It was business as usual. It seemed as if she had not been away at all. Evelyn Majakowski laughed when she saw her. "So, did Ms. Benckhoff release you already?"

Michaela made a face. "I believe I did that myself," she said. "I just couldn't stand it at home any longer."

"I'm not surprised. With that apartment," Evelyn said. "I've never seen anything like it. Don't you want to find something more like home?"

"It has always been sufficient for me," Michaela said, slightly irritated.

"Well, soon it may not be," Evelyn Majakowski stated mysteriously.

Michaela pointed towards her office. "Is my mail on my desk?"

"It's with Ms. Benckhoff," Evelyn said. "She's taking care of things now."

Michaela raised her eyebrows.

"Somebody had to do it," Evelyn Majakowski said. "You surely wouldn't have wanted it to stack up."

"No." Michaela cleared her throat. "I wouldn't have wanted that."

She went to Ramona's office. When she entered, Ramona was sitting bent over her desk, and for a moment, Michaela was happy to see her again. Ramona had not been to see her for two days, since she had been feeling better.

Ramona looked up. A smile spread across her face. "Are you feeling well again?" She got up. "You could've stayed at home a couple of days longer," she said walking towards Michaela and eying her with concern. "You don't look completely well yet."

"I'll recover faster if I work," Michaela said. "Sitting at home and doing nothing was driving me crazy."

"Oh, you workaholics!" Ramona laughed.

"I can see you're one of us now," Michaela pointed at Ramona's cluttered desk.

"Now I can give some of it back to you." Ramona smiled.

Michaela was overwhelmed by that smile, as always. She quickly stepped past Ramona and walked to the desk. "What can I take?"

Ramona followed her. "This." She took a small stack. "These require your approval."

She passed the papers to Michaela, and when Michaela took them, their fingers touched lightly. Michaela thought her fever was returning. This touch, even if it was by chance ... And the whole room was filled with Ramona's scent ... Michaela turned around quickly and left the room with the letters.

In her office, Michaela sat at her desk and stared at nothing. She could not work. She thought of Ramona's eyes, Ramona's lips, of every time they had touched during those days while Ramona had been taking care of her. Even though she still felt weak and her nose was very stuffy, when she closed her eyes, she could perceive Ramona's scent.

While she was sick, Ramona had been with her for hours. That was a thing of the past, now that she was well again. She felt a stab to her heart. She did not want it to be over. She wanted to see Ramona every day, outside of work.

Evelyn Majakowski came into the room and put a cup in front of her. "Tea," she said. "Ms. Benckhoff thought coffee wouldn't be good for you yet."

Michaela looked up at her. "Am I under surveillance?" She looked a bit reluctantly at the tea.

"You have to complain to Ms. Benckhoff about that." Evelyn raised her hands. "I'm not getting mixed up in this."

"Mixed up in what?" Michaela asked and leaned back.

Evelyn Majakowski grinned. "When I look at the two of you . . . and when I consider how often Ms. Benckhoff visited you while you were sick . . . you should – you should thank her soon by inviting her to something." Her grin grew wider, and she left Michaela's office.

Michaela stared after her. Maybe that was a good idea. She would have loved to go right back to Ramona's office again. But she did not. Instead, she sipped her tea. It was the same one Ramona had made for her at home.

She closed her eyes and dreamed a bit.

❧ ❦ ❧

Once again it was evening in the office and dark. Michaela had never gotten used to working with bright lights in the evening, so she sat in the glow of her little desk lamp and read her papers. Weeks had passed since her bout with the flu and she felt more energetic than ever before. Maybe it was the onset of spring that was slowly entering every aspect of life. People were wearing brighter colors and laughed more, everything was turning green and starting to bloom.

She heard a noise and looked up.

"You're still here, too?" Ramona asked. She was standing in the door. "I just wanted to drop off a few papers for you before I go. You need to sign them."

Michaela nodded. "Why are you still here?" she asked. "Isn't your daughter waiting for you?"

"Oh, soon she won't be needing me anymore." Ramona laughed. "She's almost so at home with the Majakowskis. She doesn't want to leave them at all." She put the papers down on the desk in front of Michaela. "The quarterly statement," she said. "Even on time for once, thanks to the new computers." She smiled.

Despite the dim lighting, Ramona's smile lit up the whole room. Michaela averted her gaze; she felt dazzled. She closed the file she had been working on. "How about we go out for dinner after such a long work day?" she asked. "Your daughter is taken care of, and I'm in no rush to get home. I had wanted to thank you for a while for taking care of me when I was sick."

"You don't have to do that," Ramona said. "That was the natural thing to do."

"I don't agree," Michaela said. She got up. "So? Yes or no?"

Ramona hesitated for a moment. Michaela was wondering why. She had been going in and out of her apartment as if it were her home already, but dinner made her hesitate?

"I . . . yes," Ramona said finally. "I'm just going to call the Majakowskis and let them know I'll be coming back later."

"Okay." Michaela put the things on her desk away. "I'll be waiting for you."

They went to the same restaurant where they had their first lunch together. This time the romantic mood Evelyn Majakowski had been talking about was apparent. It was evening and the lights were low. There were almost exclusively couples at the tables, gazing at each other in candle light.

"Spring is in the air." Ramona said once they had taken their seats. She laughed and pointed her head in the direction of a couple close by that was celebrating this particular time of year in a very intense way.

"Yes," Michaela said and used the opportunity to thoroughly study Ramona while she was looking the other direction.

When Ramona's glance returned from the neighboring table, it met Michaela's and rested a bit too long on it. Ramona cleared her throat. "Yes . . . uh . . . Shall we order?" She opened the menu and studied it, seemingly intent on avoiding another encounter with Michaela's eyes.

They ate and talked, but exclusively about work and about Leonie's progress with her therapy.

"It's really a miracle," Ramona repeated. "If I consider . . . Just a few months ago I thought she would —" She did not want to say the word out loud.

"It must have been hard for you, all those years," Michaela said. "I can't imagine the burden it must have put on you."

Ramona looked at her. "I believe you know what a burden means, albeit in a different way."

"You can't compare that," Michaela said. "The company isn't the same as a child."

"I think losing the company would've been almost as devastating for you as losing my child for me," Ramona said understandingly.

"My grandfather was – the company was so important to him. He founded it and built it up," Michaela said. She had to swallow hard thinking of her grandfather. "I couldn't just abandon that. For his sake alone."

"You loved your grandfather very much," Ramona said. Her voice sounded so tender and soft.

"Yes." Michaela swallowed again. "Yes, I did."

"You never were as tough as you pretended to be," Ramona said. "I wish I would've realized that sooner. I was always terribly afraid of you."

"Afraid? Of me?" Michaela stared at her in shock. *Please, no, don't be afraid of me,* she thought.

"I bet you still have no idea how often I wasn't at the office or how often I came late. I was constantly at the hospital. Of course, I always caught up with my work, but if Mrs. Majakowski hadn't taken care of the time sheet . . ."

"She faked your time sheet?" Michaela seemed extraordinarily bewildered. She would never have expected Evelyn Majakowski to do something like that.

Ramona looked at her a bit scared. "Maybe I shouldn't have said that. Please, don't get mad at her for it."

Michaela shook her heard. "Unbelievable, what all I didn't notice," she said. "And there I was thinking I had everything under control."

"You did. And you still do," Ramona hastened to point out. "It was just . . . She wanted to protect me. I depended on the work. For Leonie. Please . . ."

Michaela looked into Ramona's eyes and saw the fear

in it. It cut into her heart. She wanted to reassure her. "Ramona ..." she said and took Ramona's hand. "Don't worry. That's all in the past. You can't believe I would fire Mrs. Majakowski for such a good deed – or you."

"I'm relieved." Ramona took a deep breath and let out a laugh of relief. "The thing with the time sheet just slipped out. There used to be a time I would never have told you, but now ..." She looked down at Michaela's hand still holding her own.

Michaela quickly withdraw her hand.

"You don't have to do that ... Mike," Ramona said softly.

"Ramona ..." Michaela whispered. Her throat felt as tight as it had during her worst fever. Her heart was beating loudly.

Ramona leaned forward and put her own hand on Michaela's, on the one she had just pulled away. "I believe we have to reevaluate our relationship completely anyway," she said with a smile.

Michaela hardly dared to look up from the table, and Ramona's hand on hers burned like fire. "Ramona ..." she whispered. "You ... you ..." She cleared her throat. "Would you want to ... Would it be okay for you if –"

"It would be okay for me," Ramona breathed. She gently caressed Michaela's hand. "It's nice being able to touch you without being your nurse." She laughed lightly. "It was hard at times for me to hold back. But you were feeling so bad ... and at least I could be with you."

"That ... that ... Why did you never say anything?" Michaela stuttered. Finally, she looked at Ramona and sank deep, deep into her eyes.

Ramona looked at her face, studied every tiny detail with a loving glance. "I didn't have the impression that you ... that you were interested in anything like that. You always had so much to do with the company, were so committed to changing everything. That you also had a private life – most would've thought that was impossible."

"Did you also think I had no ... private life?" Michaela asked, uncertain.

"Well, to be honest ... until we met that woman on the street, your ... acquaintance," Ramona smiled a bit impishly, "I somehow assumed so."

Michaela sighed. "Actually, you were right," she said. "I didn't have one. Karina is ... was ... really only a casual acquaintance, one of a very few. The others were even more casual."

"Why?" Ramona asked. "Were you only interested in casual affairs? Or did someone disappoint you that badly?"

"No." Michaela shook her head. "Not really. I was still very young when I took over the company. I just didn't have any time anymore."

"No time for love?" Ramona smiled. "One should always have time for that."

"You did, I know," Michaela said. "You love Leonie more than anything."

"That's not the kind of love I meant," Ramona said, still smiling. "But it's true, in the last few years, that was all I had. There was really no other way."

"Wasn't there ..." Michaela swallowed. "Was there never anybody? Nobody in all that time?"

"How could there be?" Ramona asked. She shrugged her shoulders. "A hospital is not the best place to find someone special."

"But before ..." Michaela did not know how she should

phrase it. "Before Leonie got sick ..."

"Leonie was born sick," Ramona said. The memory of the shock was still evident when she was thinking of it.

Michaela saw again the scene in the hospital room she had witnessed without Ramona knowing about it. She would have loved to take Ramona into her arms and console her – even now.

"Before Leonie was born ... Well, it was different then," Ramona continued. "Of course, I used to have ... relationships." The word fell a bit restrained from her mouth.

"No happy ones?" Michaela asked. "I'm sorry." She cleared her throat. "It's none of my business."

"Not as my employer, no," Ramona said. "But if somebody named Mike were to ask me ..."

"To be honest, I never really liked that name," Michaela replied with a skeptical expression. "I like my real name even less. That's why I'm happy to be called by my last name."

Ramona laughed lightly. "But I simply can't call you Wittling," she said. "That sounds like one of those lonesome cowboys in Wild West movies who don't seem to have a first name." She leaned forward and took hold of Michaela's hand again. "I actually quite like Mike," she said softly as she looked into Michaela's eyes. "It suits you." She held Michaela's hand more tenderly and whispered, "Mike ..."

Her smile penetrated Michaela, and as always, she could not defend herself against it – and did not want to either.

"Mike ..." Ramona repeated very softly with a warm tone in her voice that Michaela had never heard before at work.

"I think we should go," Michaela said. She could barely endure the touch of Ramona's hand and her gaze. She longed for her, as she believed she had never longed for another woman before.

Ramona's smile became even more affectionate. "Your place or mine?" she asked quietly.

Michaela stared at her. She was speechless. "Uh ... I ... don't know," she finally managed to say. "Do you really think that's a good idea?"

Ramona grinned. "The best," she said. "But I'll hold it in your favor that you didn't invite me to dinner with those intentions."

"No ... uh ... no, really not," Michaela stammered.

"I want to touch you," Ramona whispered almost inaudibly. "Not just your hand."

Michaela felt hot currents flowing through her body, as if she were connected to an electric wire. "I ... I — you decide," she stuttered while she was fighting to hold back the waves.

"A reversal of roles," Ramona said. "But I don't mind. My place. Your place is too bare for my tastes. Or have you changed anything about that?"

"No. No, not yet," Michaela replied haltingly. "But ... Leonie ..."

"She can stay overnight with the Majakowskis," Ramona said. "I arranged it with Evelyn when I called her earlier."

"You ... you did that?" Michaela stared at her with an open mouth.

"Yes. Evelyn also thought that was for the best." Ramona's smile bordered on a grin.

"She thought that?" Michaela was flabbergasted.

Ramona nodded. "Evelyn was saying all the time if you

didn't get your act together soon, she'd take matters into her own hands."

Michaela just stared at her, unable to speak. This was pure conspiracy!

"Evelyn cares for you a lot," Ramona said affectionately. "Almost like she's your mother. She wants you to be happy. And she believes —" Ramona interrupted herself and looked to the side.

"She believes the two of us . . .?" Michaela regained her composure only slowly.

"Yes, that's what she believes." Ramona looked at her again. "But if you don't agree —"

Don't agree? Strong protest was instantly bubbling up inside Michaela. "What do you believe?" Michaela asked with difficulty. "Do you agree with Mrs. Majakowski?"

"I . . ." Ramona swallowed. "I never thought it possible I could have such feelings for a woman again. I was so preoccupied with Leonie that I thought everything else . . . was out of the question. It didn't hold any value anymore. And if Leonie had . . ." she brought herself to say the word out loud, "died, then maybe it would have definitely been that way."

Michaela thought of the scene in the cemetery, in front of Leonie's grave. Ramona had been alone; there was nobody at her side. Her assumption had proven to be true.

"I'm so sorry for everything you had to go through," she said. She stroked the back of Ramona's hand, turned it over and placed a kiss on the inside. "Oh, Ramona," she whispered. Ramona's skin was so warm and soft, she yearned for more.

"Please let's go," Ramona whispered urgently. "Or else I can't guarantee that I can restrain myself in public."

"But, Ms. Benckhoff …" Michaela pulled herself together and laughed lightly. "I always thought of you as such a shy person."

"Ms. Benckhoff is," Ramona said, getting up from her seat. "But this is Ramona talking."

The drive to Ramona's apartment was short, even though it was in a suburb, where the rents were lower. Just like Michaela's apartment, it had only two rooms, but Ramona's home radiated a completely different atmosphere. The walls were adorned with drawings, obviously done by a child, and photos of Leonie. Everything was decorated in bright colors and looked as if Ramona had made many things herself to decorate their modest home.

Michaela was overwhelmed by the warm, homey atmosphere that welcomed her. She glanced around and looked at Leonie's pictures while Ramona hung her coat. "You have a lovely daughter," she said.

Ramona moved to her side and together they studied a photo of Leonie that showed her beaming and holding a doll up in the air. "That was in America," she said. "When the treatment had started to work and she could go outside for the first time." She swallowed. "Until then it hadn't been clear if she —"

"Ramona …" Michaela put an arm around her.

"That's in the past now," Ramona said, wiping a tear from her eye. "Sometimes I still can't believe it."

"I'm happy Leonie is doing fine," Michaela said. "I hope to meet her someday soon."

Ramona looked up at her. She had to; the difference in height was rather substantial. "Do you really want to?" she asked anxiously. "Do you … do you like kids?"

Michaela shook her head. "Honestly, I've never really thought about it," she said. "That question never came up."

"But . . . but you could imagine liking Leonie?" Ramona inquired again.

Michaela turned to Ramona and looked directly into her eyes. "If she's like her mother," she said softly.

"Mike . . ." Ramona whispered. Her eyes roamed over Michaela's face as if she was following butterflies who could not decide where to rest.

"Ramona . . ." Michaela's voice broke slightly. "I . . . I would so much like to kiss you."

Ramona laughed quietly. "Am I stopping you?"

"No." Michaela put a hand on Ramona's cheek, ran her fingers over the soft skin, let them circle gently behind her ear. She bent down and timidly touched Ramona's lips with hers.

Ramona sighed softly. She moved closer to Michaela and embraced her. She was shaking. "Please be gentle with me," she whispered as they drew apart from the kiss. "I haven't done this for a very long time."

Michaela felt such a wave of affection that it almost overwhelmed her. "I want to give you all the tenderness in the world," she whispered and took Ramona protectively into her arms.

Ramona pressed against her, rested her head against Michaela's chest and sighed again. "I haven't felt this safe in a long time," she said quietly. She laughed without a sound; Michaela only felt the vibration at her chest. "You are so tall and strong, so wonderful to lean on."

"If you want to, feel free to do that," Michaela said. She smiled tenderly and ran her hand over Ramona's hair. "I can't imagine anything more beautiful than holding you."

"Nothing?" Ramona asked. "Does that mean you don't want more?"

"That's not what I meant," Michaela replied. "And you know it."

"Yes." Ramona leaned back and looked up to Michaela with a mischievous gleam in her eyes. "I just wanted to test you. Because I can imagine," she cleared her throat, "something more."

"Me, too," Michaela breathed. She bent down and kissed her again, this time with so much passion that she stole Ramona's breath.

"Oh my god . . ." Ramona gasped when Michaela let go of her. "I think I'm going to faint."

"I know how to prevent that," Michaela said with a smile, lifting her into her arms.

Ramona stared at her with surprise.

"I also do a few push-ups before I go jogging," Michaela said with a smirk.

"If I had known that," Ramona replied enthusiastically, "I might not have taken you with me to my apartment just like that."

"Why not?" Michaela kissed her quickly. "Push-ups are quite useful for certain activities."

"Thank goodness it's dark in here," Ramona whispered. "I think I'm turning red as a tomato."

Michaela carried her into the bedroom, the light from the hallway illuminating the room weakly. "Would you prefer no light?" Michaela asked with a whisper. She gently let Ramona slide onto the bed. "I would like to see you."

Ramona reached over to her nightstand and switched on the lamp. A soft, pastel yellow light filled the room. "Please don't laugh at me," she said. "I know I'm behaving like an old maid."

Michaela slid next to Ramona onto the bed and caressed her face. "If anything, then more like a young maid," she laughed tenderly.

"Mike ..." Ramona whispered. Her eyes searched Michaela's and she lost herself in them. "Mike ..." she whispered again. "I so much want to touch you; I can no longer bear it."

"Ramona ..." Michaela whispered the name like a prayer. Her fingers caressed Ramona's lips, down her neck and opened her blouse button by button. Her eyes never left Ramona's face. She exposed the bra and moved her hand over it.

Ramona moaned. "Oh god ... I had forgotten how nice that is," she whispered.

"Already?" Michaela laughed.

"You promised not to laugh," Ramona complained.

"I'm not." Michaela became serious. "I'm not laughing at you. It's just so nice," she swallowed, "to be with you."

Ramona looked at her with eyes as deep as the sea. She put her arms around Michaela's neck and pulled her closer. "I want to be with you always," she whispered. "Always and forever." Her lips found Michaela's mouth and kissed her gently.

Michaela was spellbound by this gentleness. She wanted Ramona, and yet, she felt it was not just desire filling her. There was a much stronger feeling, something she had not felt in a very long time. "Ramona ..." she whispered. "Darling ..."

She felt Ramona's hands roaming over her back, slipping under her shirt onto her naked skin. She moaned. She tried to control herself, despite the desire bursting open inside her like hot lava bursting through the earth's crust. Ramona's hands went lower, opened the button of her pants and the zipper, her hand slipped inside.

Michaela stopped her. "Not so fast, Ramona, please. I want to savor it. If you touch me now ..."

"I want to, so much," Ramona whispered with a husky voice. Again, her hand slipped lower.

"Don't!" Michaela jumped up and laughed. "Won't you listen to what I'm saying?"

"Not in a situation like this," Ramona said. "We're not in the office here."

Michaela smiled and shook her head and quickly undressed before lying down again.

Ramona followed her naked figure longingly with her eyes, received her gently in her arms and sighed quietly. "It's so nice to feel you," she whispered.

Michaela caressed Ramona's back and unfastened her bra, pushed it up. The gentle curves below it made her stop for a moment in admiration. She lowered herself and took one of Ramona's nipples into her mouth. It was hard. Michaela's tongue played with it, rolled it back and forth, exploring the surface that was covered with tiny dimples.

Ramona arched her back and writhed, moaning all the while. "You're going to ... drive me mad," she whispered with effort. "That's not fair."

"It's not?" Michaela grinned.

"No," Ramona groaned. "No, no, no ..."

Michaela's ran her hands down Ramona's sides while she gave lavish attention to her breasts. She enjoyed the soft skin with her lips, tongue and the tips of her fingers. It was an intoxicating feeling. She slowly pulled off Ramona's clothes in the process until she was naked. "Good thing you have a heater in your bedroom," she teased.

"Good thing," Ramona replied. "Yours ... brr!" She laughed.

Suddenly, Michaela went very still while she looked over Ramona's alabaster, gleaming body. "You are so beautiful," she whispered, overwhelmed. She ran her hand over Ramona's breast, causing Ramona to arch against her again and moan. Tenderly she moved her hand down to Ramona's belly. Her hand was tingling almost unbearably from all the wonderful sensations. Slowly, she approached the triangle leading into paradise.

"Yes." Ramona trembled. "Yes ..." She parted her legs slightly.

Michaela closed her eyes for a moment. She could almost see Ramona's delicious oyster. She longed to touch her, to taste her, to breathe the scent that she knew would enchant her forever.

"Please ..." Ramona whispered. "Touch me ..." She was breathing heavily and with effort.

"Yes, my darling," Michaela whispered and bent down to her. She could feel this night with Ramona would not be a one-time experience. She would not curse the wasted hours in the morning. This was something very special and she wished the night would last forever.

"Yes, my darling," she repeated and slipped between Ramona's legs.

❧❧❧❧

C offee for breakfast?"

Michaela opened her eyes and was confused that everything surrounding her was unfamiliar. Everything but Ramona's face, watching her with a smile.

"I ... yes ... uh ..." She looked at the clock that was standing on the very feminine looking nightstand next to her, which was far from the plain wooden cube that Michaela used for the same purpose, though she had no clock. The hands were showing — That could not be right! "Seven o'clock?" she sighed, incredulous.

"Too early? Would you like to sleep a bit longer?" Ramona laughed. "I'll switch off the coffee machine then."

"Too early?" Michaela jerked upright. "It's been years since I've slept this late!" She threw her legs over the edge of the bed and got up. "I run from half past five to six, and then I drive into the office."

Ramona grinned. "In that case, you should maybe put on some clothes first," she said and disappeared.

Michaela looked down. She was stark naked. And this was how she had presented herself to Ramona? She looked around. Her clothes were neatly stacked on a chair. She could not remember taking them off this orderly the night before. Indeed, that had been rather ... disorderly. She blushed slightly. Ramona had to have picked up already this morning, while Michaela was still sleeping.

She grabbed her clothes and dressed quickly. Then she followed the sounds and found Ramona in the kitchen. "I'm sorry," she said. "It was ... It's just been a really long time since I spent the night outside my own home."

"I was guessing that," Ramona said and let a pancake slide from the pan onto a plate. She smiled at Michaela. "Good morning."

"Oh ... uh ... Good morning." Michaela stood there, feeling awkward. "Can I help you somehow?"

"After seeing your kitchen?" Ramona looked at her with mock horror. "No way! Sit down and eat your breakfast. Everything's ready."

Michaela looked at the affectionately set table. It was a small table, as small as the kitchen. Just big enough for two. Nonetheless, Ramona had managed to find space for some decoration next to the plates, cups and food. A small flower bouquet in the middle gave the whole table a hint of spring.

"I ... I usually don't have breakfast," Michaela said in a daze, but sat down anyway.

"If you get up that early, it's even more important," Ramona criticized with motherly strictness. She came to Michaela and poured her a cup of coffee.

Michaela slowly regained her senses. She grabbed Ramona and pulled her onto her lap. "Right now, there's something much more important," she said and kissed a surprised Ramona who was unable to defend herself as she was still holding the coffee pot.

"We have to leave for the office," Ramona said. "Or we'll be late." She tried to free herself from Michaela.

"Was that the reason you fled from bed so quickly?" Michaela asked. "You must have been up for ages." She laughed a bit. "Rest assured, I can never come too late. I'm the boss and if you come in with me –"

"I don't want to ... I don't want to have an advantage from being –" Ramona twisted uncomfortably in Michaela's lap.

Michaela let her go and Ramona got up quickly. "What's up, Ramona?" Michaela asked. "What's the matter with you?"

"Nothing," Ramona said, put the coffee pot down and took a seat.

Michaela looked at her and felt everything she had been wishing for, for years. It was a very warm feeling and so beautiful. "You were incredibly sweet last night," she said softly.

"Please ... please don't," Ramona said and refused to look at her. "Let's just have breakfast and then —"

"And then?" Michaela laughed. She was thinking they could as well return to bed after breakfast as drive to the office.

"I have to ... I need time to think," Ramona said.

"To think? About what?" Michaela got up and went to Ramona on the other side of the table. She bent down. "About us?" she asked with a smile. She wanted to kiss her, but Ramona turned away. Michaela raised her eyebrows but did not say anything. She went back to her chair, sat down and looked at Ramona with forced calm. Inside, she was on high alert. She was afraid. "Did I understand anything wrong — yesterday evening and last night?" she asked. She took a sip of her coffee.

Ramona glanced at her and averted her gaze again. "It was like a high," she said. "And it was ... great. But ..."

"But?" Michaela kept the coffee cup in her hand and looked at Ramona over the rim. She tried to hide her anxiety.

"It's just — you ... we ... I need more time," Ramona said. It was apparent she was feeling uneasy.

"Did I ..." Michaela cleared her throat vigorously. "Did I force you to do anything you didn't want?"

"No." Ramona finally looked at her. With a serious expression. "No, you didn't. If anything," she smiled slightly, but the smile did not last, vanished right away again. "If anything it was me who forced her way."

"Is this maybe . . ." Michaela simply did not understand what Ramona tried to tell her. "Is this something you feel ashamed of? That you have needs – after such a long time?" She frowned.

"Needs. Yes. That's probably the problem," Ramona said. She leaned back in her chair.

"But . . . everybody has needs," Michaela said with a blank stare. "I mean, I also placed it last for a long time – or didn't notice it at all, but that's no reason to feel bad about it." She smiled at Ramona. "Especially when it was so great."

Ramona got up. "I think we're finished with breakfast," she said. "Shall we get to the office?" She took a few things off the table and put them into the fridge.

Michaela did not know what to say. Last night still resonated in her. It was indescribable holding Ramona in her arms, to kiss and caress her, her sweet sighs, her passionate devotion. She had assumed it must have been the same for Ramona. Now it seemed she was wrong. She said, "Ramona –"

"Please," Ramona raised a hand. "Let's drive to work."

Michaela took a deep breath. "If you want it this way."

Ramona just looked at her and did not say anything else.

❧ ❧ ❧ ❧

When they arrived at the office, Evelyn Majakowski approached them in the hallway. "I took Leonie to pre-school," she said to Ramona. She looked from Ramona to Michaela and back. It seemed as if she tried to suppress a smile.

"Thank you," Ramona said.

Evelyn seemed a bit confused. "The mail is on your desk," she continued, speaking to Michaela, "and Monsieur Valmont of the Boyer Vineyard has called. It seems to be urgent."

"I'll get back to him right away," Michaela said. She moved past her and, looking back over her shoulder, called out, "Would you please get him on the line for me?"

"Y-Yes," Evelyn replied slightly surprised, but she turned around and followed Michaela.

When Michaela finished the call, Evelyn Majakowski entered her room as she did every morning with a cup of coffee and put it down in front of her. Instead of leaving, though, she remained rooted to the spot.

Michaela looked at her. "Is something the matter?"

"That's what I'm asking you," Evelyn said.

Michaela stared contemplatively into thin air for a while. "I don't know what's up, either" she said, while her eyes returned slightly desperate to Evelyn Majakowski.

"You —" Evelyn cleared her throat discreetly. "You didn't arrive this morning together by coincidence, or am I wrong?"

"No." Michaela frowned. "You're not wrong."

"When Ramona called yesterday and asked if Leonie could stay the night —"

"She directly asked for that?" Michaela interrupted her. Surprise showed in her eyes.

"Yes. I ... I mean, it seemed like a sure —" Evelyn Majakowski appeared slightly unsure.

"Did it?" Michaela asked. "Not for me." *But obviously for Ramona,* she thought. *So why is she now so ...?* She shook her head.

"Don't mind me saying so, Michaela," Evelyn Majakowski began, "but you stalked around each other like two tigers in the jungle."

"Was it so conspicuous?" Michaela got up and walked over to her liquor shelf. She grabbed a bottle of Cognac and looked at it as if nothing else could interest her anymore.

"It was so inconspicuous that it was conspicuous," Evelyn Majakowski said. "Just like this morning."

Michaela sighed. "If you want to know what happened you have to ask Ramona," she remarked. "I can't tell you." She put the bottle back on the shelf and returned to her desk.

"But something has to be wrong," Evelyn said. "After the call yesterday, I had thought you two would be arriving here on cloud nine this morning."

"I would have thought the same," Michaela said. "Until breakfast." She sat down and raised her hands, perplexed. "Ask Ramona. I have no idea what it could be."

"You didn't do anything?" Evelyn Majakowski's voice sounded apprehensive.

Michaela looked at her indignantly. "Nothing she didn't want. What do you think of me?"

Evelyn made a slight grimace. "I'm sorry, that was inconsiderate of me."

"No, you are right." Michaela sighed again. "If you con-sider how I've been behaving for the past couple of years . . ."

"Thank goodness that's in the past," Evelyn Majakow-ski said. "But apparently there are different kinds of problems now."

"Apparently," Michaela confirmed.

Evelyn started, "I so much wish for you and Ramona –"

"I've already heard about your wish," Michaela inter-rupted her slightly irked.

"Ramona shouldn't have told you," Evelyn Majakowski retorted, "but still, I stand behind it. After all, I've known you since your birth, and you can't change any-thing about that." She smiled and left the room.

Michaela did not see Ramona all day. It was as if she had barricaded herself in her office. When Michaela wanted to ask her out to lunch around midday, she was already gone. When she returned, Michaela had to go to a meet-ing. This way it turned evening before Michaela could even think of having a private word with her.

She walked to Ramona's office and stood for a moment undecided in front of the closed door. Should she go in or not? What if Ramona expected her to be more re-served, what if she felt pressured? Michaela sighed. She had to do this; it could not be avoided.

She assertively pressed down on the door handle. Ra-mona was sitting at her desk and working. She looked up when Michaela entered the room and did not show any emotion. Michaela closed the door. "Ramona," she said.

Ramona did not reply. She simply looked at Michaela.

Michaela moved to Ramona's desk and stopped in

front of it. "If I hurt you in any way, please tell me," she appealed. "If I did anything wrong –"

Ramona still did not say anything.

"Ramona," Michaela begged, "please don't just leave me standing in the rain. What is the matter?"

Ramona got up and walked over to the window. She crossed her arms, turned around and looked out. After a while, she turned around again and looked at Michaela. "Did you promote me to head of bookkeeping because you were after me?" she asked.

Michaela stared at her as if struck by lightning. "Wh– What? I beg your pardon?"

"You heard me," Ramona answered cool. "There was no particular reason to promote me. There are others with more seniority. So, why did you do it? It came very . . . unexpectedly."

Michaela stood there, taken by surprise. What should she tell Ramona? That it was all down to the ghosts? She pulled herself together. "You deserved it," she said as calmly as possible, "for purely business reasons."

"Purely business reasons." Ramona repeated thoughtfully and returned to her desk.

"You are the best person for the position, I told you before," Michaela explained. "I had not promoted anybody for years, and we needed a head of bookkeeping. That was all."

"That was all," Ramona repeated again.

"Ramona . . ." Michaela rounded the desk and stopped in front of her. "What's all this about? Why are you so upset? Everything seemed okay last night." She tentatively caressed Ramona's cheek.

Ramona stepped back to move out of her reach. "Last night, I let myself go," she said.

Michaela would have loved to shake her head – and Ramona, too. She could not believe any of this. "Do you regret it?" she asked.

"I . . . I don't regret it. It was wonderful," Ramona said haltingly. "I just don't want my job to depend on me –"

"On you sleeping with me?" Michaela gave an incredulous laugh. "Do you seriously believe that?"

"I have to think of Leonie," Ramona said. "It's not just about me."

"Yes, it is," Michaela said. "It is about you, only about you." She stepped closer again and looked at her directly. "Leonie will be able to go to a private school if you want. I can take care of that – and I'd like to. We can make a contract for it. Some kind of trust or something like it. Completely independent from anything that's happening between us – or not happening." She tried to catch Ramona's eyes but failed.

"You would do that?" Ramona asked, stepped aside and moved passed her.

"Of course, I would do that!" Michaela followed her and stopped behind her. "I would do anything for you – and Leonie is a part of you." She carefully put her hands on Ramona's shoulders. "Please," she said softly, "tell me what's on your mind."

Ramona stood still for a moment, then she took a few steps and moved away from Michaela. "Let's talk about this later," she said. "Please."

Michaela took a deep breath. "As you wish," she said. She felt disappointment rise in her. "Then we'll let it be." Annoyed, she stormed out of Ramona's office and slammed the door behind her.

A few days passed. Ramona and Michaela did not speak to each other. They met in the hallway, greeted each other quickly, and walked past one another. Sometimes, when Michaela was leaving her office, she had the feeling Ramona's door was closing, as if Ramona had just wanted to do the same but refrained from doing so to avoid an accidental meeting.

Michaela could still not figure out what had happened. She had played the night over and over in her mind – with some hot consequences for her inner feelings – also the evening before it and the morning after, but she could not find anything that would have explained Ramona's cold attitude. Had she not done enough? Even the trust for Leonie . . . It simply remained a mystery.

She shook her head and concentrated on her files again. That is, she tried to. She still felt Ramona's inexplicable rejection nagging at her, just like she had every day. It was like a vase that had been lying shattered in pieces for a long time, and in that one night, all the pieces had joined again, as if by magic. Then it was standing on the mantelpiece in all its shining glory, complete and visible to everybody. Now, there was a big ugly hole where a piece was missing in the front, and she did not know where to find it.

"Mike? Could you please take at look at this?" Ramona entered the office, did not look at Michaela but right away pushed a folder under her nose.

Michaela felt like suddenly being torn from one life into another. She cleared her throat to regain her composure. "Mike?"

"Oh . . . uh . . . Do you prefer Michaela?" Ramona was thrown by her remark. "Or Ms. Wittling?" She made a face.

"No, that's not necessary," Michaela said. "Just keep calling me Mike. It just ... caught me off guard." Her heart was pounding loudly, because Ramona was so close to her for the first time in days.

Ramona closed the folder and pressed it to her chest under her folded arms.

Michaela got up. "I like how you say Mike," she remarked with a smile. She now stood very close to Ramona and could see into her eyes.

Ramona lowered her gaze. "Mike, please," she said quietly. She raised her eyes again up to Michaela. "I can't talk to you privately now. I just needed to ask you something." Her voice became steadier. "We have to work together and –" She smiled shyly. "Do you remember? 'I hope it won't be a burden on our professional relationship' – those were your own words."

"Under slightly different circumstances, though," Michaela said and looked inquisitively at Ramona. There was something in her voice that gave her hope.

"The circumstances have changed, I know," Ramona said. "And I'm not without blame. But still ..."

"Ramona ..." Michaela said softly. She studied Ramona's face. "We can't continue to beat around the bush forever. I don't know what's wrong. You need to tell me."

"Mike, please ..." Ramona's voice sounded pained. She searched Michaela's eyes.

"Michaela? Do you have –" Evelyn Majakowski suddenly stood in the door. "Oh, I'm sorry," she interrupted herself when she saw Michaela and Ramona standing so close to each other.

Ramona reacted immediately. She pushed the folder into Michaela's arms, turned around and quickly left the room without looking at Evelyn Majakowski.

Evelyn Majakowski stared confusedly after her. Then she entered Michaela's office.

Michaela put the folder down onto her desk contemplatively, sat down and opened it.

"I assume I'm not to ask anything again," Evelyn Majakowski remarked.

Michaela sighed. "Yes, that's the way it goes. You can change everything but people. Especially not those ..." she faltered. "Especially not those you care about."

"Did you tell her that?"

"What?" Michaela asked.

"That you care about her," Evelyn said.

"But that ... that goes without saying," Michaela replied confused. "After all, we had —"

"That's no substitute," Evelyn interrupted. "Did you tell her you love her? Or were you thinking you'd show it to her by having sex?"

"Uh ..." Michaela was speechless. She was able to answer only after a while. "Do you really think that could be it?"

Evelyn breathed out a deep sigh. "Children ..." she said leniently. "I've gotten to know Ramona very well in the past few months. The love for Leonie has determined her whole life — ever since Leonie was born. She is a woman who loves very deeply. So she's also expecting it of others." She tilted her head. "Do you love her?" she asked. "Or was it really just a —"

"No!" Michaela protested vehemently. "Ramona also accused me of that. How does the whole world come up with the idea I'm only after sex? Do I look like that?" She raised her head and gave Evelyn Majakowski a questioning look.

"Well ..." Evelyn Majakowski shrugged her shoulders. "You can't ask me that. To me, you're more like a daughter. I don't think about you in those terms."

"I of all people ..." Michaela shook her head, with still utter disbelief. "Do you have any idea how often in the past few years I even –"

Evelyn interrupted her with a raised hand. "I don't even want to know!" She laughed. "Don't take it the wrong way, but that's your private business." She turned serious again. "But I do know how much you used to work and how late you left in the evenings, or nights, I should say. And how early you were there in the mornings. It's clear to me that there was not much room for a private life."

"Hardly any," Michaela said. She got up. "Thank you very much, Mrs. Majakowski. You really helped me a lot."

She left her office, and Evelyn bent down to the desk to find the answer to the question she had wanted to ask when she had come in.

Michaela entered Ramona's office without knocking. Enough with the games. The matter had to be resolved once and for all. "Ramona ..." she started forcefully. Then she noticed that Ramona was staring at her desk and did not even seem to have noticed her presence. She frowned.

Finally, Ramona looked up. "What is this?" she asked, holding up a piece of paper.

Michaela came closer and just glanced at the paper. "A check," she said unappreciatively and turned away again, uninterested.

"Did you sign it?" Ramona asked.

Michaela glanced at the paper again. "Yes, of course," she said. "Why are you asking? You know my signature."

"I just wanted to make sure," Ramona said. "The check just arrived as acknowledgement from an American bank."

Michaela winced inwardly. She knew she had to come up with something, and fast. Her thoughts were racing. "The wine from California —"

"Mike!" Ramona interrupted her. "Don't lie to me! Do you really think in my position I could not trace where that money went and for what purpose?"

Michaela did not know what to say. She tried to remain calm. "I had thought that one would've been settled long ago," she said.

"It was." Ramona got up. "If the American banks didn't have the habit of sending out all that stuff again at the end of the quarter, I would never have learned about it."

"And you were not supposed to either," Michaela said.

Ramona looked at her. "Why not?" she asked softly. "You saved Leonie's life." Her voice quivered.

"That . . ." Michaela cleared her throat. "That was all I wanted."

"Why?" Ramona asked once more. "You didn't even know her."

Those damn ghosts! Michaela swore internally. Ramona would never believe what really happened. "But I knew you," she said.

Ramona gave a laugh. "You hardly knew my name!"

"Mrs. Majakowski had told me how bad Leonie was doing."

Ramona came closer and looked into her face, searching her eyes. "And I thought you —"

Michaela pulled her close. "I love you, Ramona," she

said. She kissed her hair. "I love you so much."

Ramona seemed stunned for a moment, then she rested her head on Michaela's chest and sighed. "I love you too, Mike," she whispered. "If it hadn't been for the worry about Leonie I might have loved you from the first moment."

"Such a monster as I was?" Michaela laughed.

"You were no monster, never," Ramona said and looked up to her. "You were just hiding behind a mask."

"A mask that sparked fear and terror in you. I am so terribly sorry about that," Michaela said sadly. "I never should've been that way."

"But you did, you had to." Ramona pulled back slightly and looked at her. "You had to rescue the company." She smiled. "You are a big knight in shining armor."

"Stop it!" Michaela laughed self-consciously. "You're embarrassing me."

"That's sweet." Ramona grinned. "I want to thank you," she said, turning serious. "I will be thankful to you my whole life for what you did. If Leonie had died –"

"Shhh." Michaela put a finger on Ramona's lips. "Nothing about that anymore. I don't want you to be grateful to me. Let's just forget about it, as if it never happened. Leonie is healthy now. That's the only thing that matters."

"Mike ..." Ramona raised her hand and softly traced a finger over Michaela's face. "Mike ..." she repeated quietly.

Michaela leaned down to her and kissed her tenderly.

"Ramona, I can't –" Evelyn Majakowski stood in the door Michaela had not closed behind her.

Michaela and Ramona finished the kiss, looked at Evelyn but did not move away from each other. They stayed closely embraced.

"Somehow I have bad timing today," Evelyn snickered. "Don't let me disturb you, children, just continue," she said and disappeared.

Michaela and Ramona laughed. "She really is the soul of the company, in every way," Ramona said.

Michaela nodded. "Yes, that's right. I don't know what would've become of me if she hadn't –" She looked at Ramona. "And before you kick me out again, ask for a time-out or something like that: I want to get to know Leonie!"

"Right now?" Ramona stared at her.

"Yes, exactly. Right now."

"She's in pre-school," Ramona said.

"Is that an obstacle?" Michaela asked. She took Ramona by the hand and pulled her out of the office.

Epilogue

In a big house just outside the city, the candles were sparkling on the tree and casting a comfortable light.

A small family sat next to it, the little girl unwrapped presents, and the two adults watched her with smiles on their faces.

"Not so fast, sweetheart," Ramona said. She ran a hand over Leonie's hair. "The presents are all yours. Nobody will take them away from you."

Leonie did not even glance up. She was much too busy tearing open paper and waiting with eyes blazing to discover what might be revealed. Adults always had to make it so exciting. Could they not just give presents without all the wrapping?

"I believe we're unnecessary here right now," Michaela said with a smile.

"I agree." Ramona sighed and got up from crouching down. "It's her first real Christmas – outside of the hospital and with so many presents. I was never able to afford –"

"Shhh. Don't think about the past," Michaela said. She wrapped her arms around Ramona. "That's long gone and won't return."

Ramona leaned against her. "It's still hard for me to grasp at times." She looked up at Michaela. "That you're here, with me . . . and Leonie. It's like a dream."

"Keep dreaming, darling," Michaela said with a smile. She caressed Ramona gently and hugged her close. "It can't hurt to dream a bit." *That might have helped me back then, too,* she thought. She led Ramona to the couch, and they both sat down. "You haven't even looked for your own presents yet," she said.

"My own presents?" Ramona frowned and looked at Michaela. "Didn't I forbid you to give me anything? We agreed on that. You've already done so much for us –"

Michaela smiled. "There are some presents that can't be refused, I'm afraid," she said. She lifted a cushion from the couch and pulled out a small box. "Like this, for example." She handed the colorfully wrapped box to Ramona.

Ramona looked at it, took it and shook her head at Michaela. "I should've known that you wouldn't stick to our agreement. When do you ever stick to something you don't like?"

Michaela laughed. "Guilty as charged," she said. She looked at Ramona expectantly. "Don't you want to open it?"

Ramona put the box on the table. "Maybe tomorrow," she said.

"Ramona!" Michaela grabbed the box. "Well, then I'll do it." She quickly removed the wrapping paper, opened the box and took out something. She took hold of Ramona's hand and knelt down. "Will you marry me?" she asked and pushed the ring over Ramona's finger.

At first, Ramona stared at the twinkling jewel on her hand, then she stared speechless at Michaela. "That . . . that . . . What are you doing?" she finally stammered after the room had been filled for a while with nothing but the rustling of paper from Leonie unwrapping her presents.

"What does it look like?" Michaela asked.

"This is . . ." Ramona wiggled the hand with the ring in front of her eyes. "That's much too expensive," she said, moved.

Michaela was still kneeling in front of her. "How can anything be too expensive – for the woman of my life?" She smiled. "For the woman I love?"

Ramona turned her gaze from the sparkling diamond to Michaela. "Don't you want to get up?" she asked. "Please, get up."

Michaela shook her head. "I'm waiting for an answer," she explained. "I can't get up before that."

"That's blackmail," Ramona said. "After all, I can't leave you kneeling there for the rest of your life."

"Well, I hope not," Michaela said.

"I . . . I don't know what to say." Ramona glanced from Michaela to the ring and back.

"You don't know? Is it so difficult?" Michaela looked at her with alarm. "Are you not sure?"

"Oh yes, I . . ." Ramona studied Michaela's face. "I love you. I'm certain about that. No doubt about it."

"How nice," Michaela said. "Same here. So, what is it then?"

"It's . . . I . . . getting married?" Ramona seemed unsure. "I have never thought about it."

"Then please think about it now," Michaela said. She held on to Ramona's hand with both of hers. "I love you. I want to be with you. I want you to be my wife. For the whole world and officially. Not just here at home."

Ramona chuckled. "But everybody already knows!"

"At work, yes," Michaela said. "It would hardly have been possible to hide it, seeing that we are both there every day. That's not enough for me. I want more."

Ramona looked at her. "You always do," she said softly. "You always want everything and immediately."

"I've waited almost nine months!" Michaela replied indignantly. "You can hardly call that *immediately*."

"That's a long time for you, isn't it?" Ramona's smile became tender. "You are so wild, so untamed — like a leopard in the wild, no, a black panther." She ran her hand over Michaela's hair that gleamed like ebony in the candle light. "Like a beast of prey following the call of the jungle."

Michaela looked at her aghast. "That's how you see me?"

"I don't think I'm the only one," Ramona whispered lovingly.

"I'm the perfectly harmless boss in a perfectly harmless little company," Michaela said with irritation. "Nothing else."

Ramona laughed. "You're anything but harmless."

"No?" Michaela knit her brows.

"You are sweet." Ramona's voice sounded soft and familiar. "You are so very sweet." Her eyes filled with tears. "Just a year ago ... on Christmas Eve ... I would never have thought possible what's happening here today, what has been happening all year —"

"I ... I wouldn't have either." Michaela swallowed. She had almost forgotten about it, but suddenly all the images were back in her mind. The images of that night when so much had happened.

"Could we —" Ramona cleared her throat. "Could we maybe postpone it still a little bit?"

Michaela's disappointment over Ramona's lacking enthusiasm showed clearly on her face. "What? The wedding? How long do you want to postpone it? Till doomsday?"

"No, I ..." Ramona seemed torn.

A smile started to spread across Michaela's face. "I'd like to quote one of your favorite sentences: It's not just about you, it's also about Leonie."

"Leonie?" Ramona did not understand.

"Yes." Michaela breathed deeply. "As should be easily observed, I have no children, but a company. A company needs heirs. Or an heiress, in this case. I would love to adopt Leonie and leave the company to her. If she wants to."

"You want to leave ... the company ... Leonie ..." Ramona trailed off, her jaw dropping.

"If she wants it" Michaela repeated. "Of course, it could be she'll prefer a career as a punk-rocker. No way to know that yet."

"Yes ... uh ..." Ramona seemed completely overwhelmed. The choice between a company heiress and a punk-rocker was too much.

"Ramona, please." Michaela put both hands on Ramona's shoulders and searched her eyes. "Say yes. I would like to give my name to you both. That would be the most beautiful Christmas present for me."

"Both of us? Your name?" Ramona could barely utter those few words.

"Well, we could of course rename the company Wittling & Benckhoff," Michaela said. "Then Leonie wouldn't have to take my name." She sighed. "You neither. If you don't want to."

"But I …" A lonely tear ran down Ramona's cheek. "But I do," she said softly. "It's all too much for me. But, I do want to. I want to so much." She gave Michaela a tender look. "So much," she repeated.

Michaela breathed deeply and got up. "So they won't have to scrape the Wittling name from the facade after all," she said quietly and happily.

"What? What did you just say?" Ramona looked at her, confused.

"Oh, nothing," Michaela said. "It doesn't matter." She paused for a moment. "It's so wonderful it can't be real." She sat down next to Ramona. "I love you," she said tenderly. She leaned forward and kissed Ramona devotedly.

"You're always smooching!" Leonie's little voice tore them back from their dream.

"It is very nice," Ramona said, turning to Leonie with a smile. "You'll come to appreciate it once you're old enough."

"Nah," Leonie protested resolutely. "That's totally yucky, all that slobbering." Then her attention was completely focused on the next present.

"Did you hear what your daughter just said?" Michaela

asked, looking deeply into Ramona's eyes.

Ramona smiled at her. "I heard it, but I don't believe it," she said. She kissed Michaela again, and everything around her sank into a bright sea of colors.

The evening went on with Leonie's excited joy over the presents. She even allowed Michaela and Ramona to play with her. So the train choo-chooed along – that is, Michaela choo-chooed and the train simply drove on its little tracks, and several stuffed animals were allowed to take turns riding it, until Leonie couldn't stop yawning, and Ramona put a stop to it all.

"It's late," she said. "Leonie has to go to bed."

Michaela nodded. "Yes, it's rather late for her."

Leonie protested. "I'm a big girl!" she said, and yawned immediately so wide that the train could have run through her mouth like a tunnel.

"Yes, you are very big." Ramona got up and picked Leonie up. "And big girls have to see to it that they get their beauty rest."

Michaela laughed. "Listen to your mother. It worked in her case."

Ramona shook her head. "You're impossible."

"Am not." Michaela grinned. "I just call it like I see it."

"Night, Mike." Leonie tiredly lifted her little hand and waved.

"Night, sweetie." Michaela walked over and kissed Leonie lovingly on the cheek. "Sweet dreams, full of all the colorful things."

Leonie glanced one more time at the Christmas tree. "We gonna play train again tomorrow?" she asked, struggling to keep her eyes open.

"Of course," Michaela said. "The whole day long, if you want to."

"She won't likely stick with one thing for so long." Ramona smiled. "With all those presents." She shook her head. "Trains. You'd think she's your child, not mine. All the dolls are lying in the corner."

Michaela scrunched up her face with a slightly guilty look. "It's not my fault. She picked it herself."

Ramona nodded. "I know. What's going to come of this? You've known each other for less than a year."

Exactly one year, Michaela thought, but she did not say anything.

Ramona looked at her daughter who was slumped in her arms now. "Now it's really high time for bed," she said. She went upstairs with Leonie.

Michaela looked outside onto the white snow that enchanted the land. It was so nice to have a home, a real home, with a woman waiting for her to come home. Well, it was not really that way. She laughed at herself. Most of the time, Ramona and she came home from work together.

It was still nice – even nicer. They saw each other all day long, then spent every night together. Their love for each other determined their lives. Just like the love for Leonie. Michaela had never had any dealings with children before Leonie had entered her life. Now she could not imagine a life without her. She could even imagine having more children, but Ramona had said no to that so far. She still had not recovered from the strain of the past years. It was also the fear of having the same thing happen again that kept her from giving in to her own wishes of having another child. She had always wanted to have a house full of children, and this was, in a way, still her intention.

Michaela smiled. It was really a dream, this life. Even if

she had not been able to buy back her grandfather's house. She had tried to, but the current owner did not want to sell. Maybe it was for the better. That way the move into this house, together with Ramona and Leonie, had been a completely new beginning.

Was she just imagining it or was there movement outside, a light in addition to that spread by the small candles on the Christmas tree in front of the window? Michaela looked closer. She could not see very much. Again, it seemed as if there was movement.

She went to the front door and stepped outside. Was somebody visiting them, in the middle of the night? There was no sound; it was still like every winter night that was illuminated just by the moon.

When she stepped down into the garden, the snow crunched beneath her feet, and the sound seemed to reverberate in the air and fill the silence, until it ebbed away.

Michaela looked out into the darkness and wondered if her perception was playing tricks on her or if somebody really was outside on this cold night. "Don't you want to come inside?" she asked out loud and felt pretty silly. "I'd have a drink for you to warm up."

No answer. No sound.

Michaela shook her head. It must have been her imagination after all. She turned around when she suddenly noticed a movement out of the corner of her eyes. Quickly she spun around again. "Oh, it's you," she said. Her heart was thumping loudly; she had been startled. She looked up along the tall dark figure. "Well, how about it?" She chuckled and pointed towards the house. "Looks a little bit different than what you were showing me back then, doesn't it?" She waved her hand dismissively. "Oh, right, you don't talk." She grinned. "But it's nice of you to come by one more time. Now I can thank you. I thank you for everything you did for me — and those two others, too. Maybe you'll meet them, and then you can tell them." She started to feel cold and rubbed her arms. She raised a hand in greeting. "Well, fare thee well then, my silent friend."

"You are most welcome," the Ghost of Christmas Future replied and rolled soundlessly away.

Baffled, Michaela followed him with her eyes. He dissolved into the darkness.

Michaela went back into the house and closed the door. "Brr!" she said.

"What were you doing outside? With no jacket or coat?" Ramona came down the stairs. "It's terribly cold outside."

"Yes, it is." Nevertheless, Michaela smiled.

"What's up?" Ramona asked, slightly confused. "Did you see something funny outside?"

"No, nothing funny," Michaela said, still smiling. "It's just that I'm a bit surprised. The lame can walk, the blind can see, and the mute can speak when you least expect it."

Ramona frowned. "I didn't understand a single word," she said.

"That's okay," Michaela said. "I just said good-bye to a friend who gave me the best Christmas present of my life."

She looked around and saw a picture of Leonie, Ramona, and the Christmas tree, all beaming at her.

The End

An excerpt from
Forbidden Passion
by
Ruth Gogoll

The small letters danced across the monitor before Kim's eyes. She gently massaged her eyelids. Working with the computer for hours was none too relaxing. However, when the exhaustion grew too great, there was this particular website on the Internet she had a habit of visiting to ease her sore eyes. It was a website full of stories; she enjoyed reading them. They were very special stories. Stories by women for women.

Slowly, Kim slid into the narrative. The woman with the chestnut-colored hair let herself fall gently onto the sofa, the other woman bent over her —

"Ms. Wolff?"

Kim spun round. Her boss stood in the door. Her chestnut-colored hair caressed her shoulders, sleek and seductive. Kim gulped.

"Is there something urgent you're working on?" her boss asked her. "Or could you spare a minute to come with me?"

"I . . . I can come," Kim stuttered arduously. And it was true. She probably could have come along with her right away.

Sonja Kantner, the department chief, and the main protagonist of Kim's fantasies of sleepless nights, gazed at the monitor. But she was too far away, the screen stood too slanted and the letters were too small. Kim thanked all goddesses in heaven for that.

"I'll just save this," Kim said, feeling hot all over. Hopefully she hadn't turned red as a tomato. But in reality she never did. She was lucky that way. Certainly it was lucky at this very moment.

"You do that," Sonja Kantner said, nodding, and turning to leave.

Kim watched her luscious bottom leave the room. Why was this woman so attractive? It was pure torture every day.

Six weeks earlier

The first time Kim had seen her new boss – at a meeting in the conference room – she had nearly fainted. She immediately created a plan to relocate the department chief's office from its strategically convenient place next to her own office to the end of the corridor – or to another floor. Best of all, to another building.

"Why don't you introduce yourself to us, Ms. Kantner," the head manager said, after offering an oral curriculum vitae of his new department chief, himself.

He retreated and Sonja Kantner stepped forward. She briefly repeated what he had already said about her, but that didn't interest Kim much. What interested her was said right at the beginning: married, without children.

"Not yet, that is," she had added with a charming smile.

The guess couldn't have been better. Kim almost sighed at the confirmation of what she had actually known already. Sonja Kantner was straight, very straight. But would it have changed anything if it hadn't been that way? Kim began stewing over her plan of having the woman relocated to another building. Weren't there foreign branch offices, too? Couldn't Sonja Kantner work there?

Kim knew one thing for sure: she wouldn't last long having Sonja Kantner right next to her, every day, nearly every minute. What was the solution? Perhaps Kim could get used to her; perhaps her desires would deaden? Kim eyed Sonja Kantner's body from top to bottom once again while she spoke. No. No, that was not going to happen. The opposite was more probable.

The meeting came to an end; Kim was on the verge of leaving when the highest-ranking manager waved to her. "Ms. Wolff? Do you have a second or two to spare?"

Kim took a deep breath and straightened her shoulders. Now she had to be brave. She walked toward the two and he introduced her with a smile. "Ms. Kantner, this is Ms. Wolff. She's going to be your closest coworker."

Sonja Kantner smiled, too, and shook Kim's hand. Kim would have preferred not touching the woman's hand at all, but she couldn't very well refuse. Sonja Kantner's palm felt soft and warm. Kim didn't ever want to let go, but Ms. Kantner withdrew it herself after the appropriate amount of time that proper manners dictated.

"I'm glad to meet you, Ms. Wolff," she said. "I hope we'll both profit from working together."

Working together? Kim repeated that silently, but she said what was expected of her: "I hope so too. I'm looking forward to it very much." She smiled sanguinely and hoped it seemed genuine. The tingling sensation spreading from her hand through her entire body prevented her from having full control of her own reactions.

"You'll take Ms. Kantner for a walk through the firm and show her around, won't you, Ms. Wolff?" her boss assumed. His tone was a friendly command.

Kim tried not to gulp. "Yes, certainly," she replied, desperately composed; her voice was very quiet. "Of course. I'll show her around." If only that had been possible! There was so much Kim would have loved to show this woman . . .!

Sonja Kantner laughed. "We'll save that for tomorrow. Today is my walk-through of the executive floor."

The boss melted in reaction to her charming smile, his reaction as strong as Kim's; yet only he was allowed to show it openly. Kim was not. *A day's grace! At least something positive!*

"I'll see you tomorrow, then," Sonja Kantner said to Kim. "What time will you be here in the morning?"

"No later than eight," Kim muttered.

"Fine," Ms. Kantner said with a smile. "I'll be here at seven."

∽৪৵

"**O**h, this really wasn't necessary, Ms. Wolff," Ms. Kantner said, beaming.

In such a good mood so early in the morning – what was to become of that! When had she gotten out of bed? Kim had been perfectly on time but Ms. Kantner was already sitting at her desk as Kim entered the office.

She made her way toward Kim to shake hands. "Good morning," she said. There was an irresistible gleam in her eyes; Kim could have sunk into them and drowned in their depths.

She probably had no idea how that affected Kim . . .

how *she* affected Kim.

"You could have come at eight on the dot," Ms. Kantner continued. "I know it gets on everyone's nerves, but I'm in the habit of catching up on work in peace and quiet in the morning. You know, before everyone else arrives. You don't get any of that done otherwise." Her laugh was unbelievably pleasant.

She had barely begun. What work did she have to catch up on? Kim forced an understanding smile to her lips and withdrew the hand Ms. Kantner was still holding. "You're absolutely right," she agreed. "I prefer doing that in the evening after everyone's left for the day."

Sonja Kantner laughed again and returned to her desk. "We all have preferences of our very own, don't we?" she said. She turned around to face Kim. "How long are you usually in the office after working hours, then?" she asked.

"Sometimes until ten, but in the morning, I usually arrive at —" She stopped in mid-sentence. Perhaps it was better her boss didn't know exactly when she used to arrive in the morning.

Sonja Kantner smiled. She was too intelligent a woman to be tricked that easily. "You're not here at seven or eight, are you?"

Kim sighed. "Well, no," she said. "But I'll change that, of course," she added hastily. "If you're here by seven, I'll be here too."

"Oh, no; that's not necessary, really," replied Sonja Kantner. "As I said: I know I get on everyone's nerves starting work so early, but I don't expect the same of anybody else." She smiled again. "I'm usually in bed by ten in the evening, though. We should strive to find a time in between."

In bed? Kim eyed her over. She was already attractive in daylight — how seductive must she look lying in her bed? She was sure to have wonderful lingerie for the nights . . . or perhaps she actually wore nothing at all . . .?

"What time could you be here by . . . at the earliest?" Sonja Kantner asked, turning the pages of a document file her predecessor had left behind.

Kim had to put an abrupt end to her thoughts first. "Half past eight, perhaps?" she suggested. She'd be able to make that. Barely.

Sonja Kantner looked up. "Fine," she finally said. Then she smiled an unbelievably likeable, almost loving smile. "And I won't say a word if that occasionally turns into nine. I guess that was what you actually wanted to suggest, wasn't it?"

She must have gone through a vast number of leadership seminars to have reached this level. "Yes," Kim admitted.

"We'll manage together somehow!" Sonja Kantner said, a laugh in her voice. "Well, will you give me that tour of the company, now?"

Together — what a nice thing to imagine, Kim mused, as Sonja Kantner proceeded out of the office ahead of her.

An excerpt from
The L Jungle
by
Ruth Gogoll

At Sappho

"**Y**ou're not serious!" Sabrina's eyes flew open. "She was there when you got home?"

"She's got a lot of nerve," said Carolin.

"I . . ." Anita wrung her hands and looked at the floor. "I can't just send her away."

"Why not?" Sabrina shook her head. "After all the liberties she's taken with you, I thought you'd finally figured this out."

"She . . . she needs me," Anita said softly. "She said so."

"Is that a new record, or has it been playing for awhile now?" Carolin sighed.

"One cappuccino, one latte, and one fresh-squeezed vitamin bomb," Melly smiled as she set down their order.

"What would you say, Melly?" Carolin asked. "Marlene showed up at Anita's place again . . . after not being around for a week."

"Right, she hasn't been around here, either." Even though Melly nodded as she spoke, she didn't appear particularly interested.

"We have to do something," Carolin said.

"About Marlene?" Melly laughed. "She's not all that

bad. You just have to let her know the score."

Sabrina raised an eyebrow. Melly headed back to the counter. Sabrina got up and walked after her. "You had something with Marlene, too?" she asked.

Melly shrugged. "When I first came to the café, a long time ago," she said.

Sabrina involuntarily glanced at Melly's ample breasts, clearly visible under her tight, sleeveless top.

Melly laughed. "Yes, that's what she's into." She glanced over at the table. "Of course I can't compete with Anita."

"Why . . ." Sabrina frowned. "Why would you take up with her?"

"Oh, she has a certain . . . robust charm," Melly replied with a laugh.

"Charm? Marlene?" Sabrina looked dumbfounded.

"I don't think she was as unhappy then as she is now. She was still working as a truck driver, so she only came in now and then."

"Chris told me that she used to drive trucks."

"That was her dream job. Ever since they took away her driver's license, though, she's stuck in an office. I think that's what makes her so short-tempered," Melly offered.

"Why did they take away her driver's license?"

"What do you think?" Melly rolled her eyes.

"Alcohol?"

"Yes, of course. She drinks way too much." Melly took a couple of bottles out of the refrigerator and began to mix a cocktail. "I told her as much, too, but she listens to no one when it comes to that subject."

"I don't think you can get her to listen when it comes to any subject," Sabrina said. She glanced over at Anita, who was talking with Carolin.

"I wouldn't say that." Melly filled the cocktail shaker with ice. "You just have to find the right starting point with her."

Sabrina laughed skeptically. "And how do you find that? Maybe I can give Anita some sort of tip."

"Anita . . ." Melly looked over at the table. "There's no sense in that. Women like Anita are deadly for Marlene. They bring out the worst in her."

Sabrina stared at her, speechless, for a moment. "You're telling me it's Anita's fault?" she finally managed in stunned disbelief.

"No one is at fault; that's not what I said," Melly countered. She decorated the cocktail and delivered it to a table.

Still mulling things over, Sabrina returned to Carolin and Anita.

"Take the key away from her," she heard Carolin say.

"I can't do that." Anita's forehead was furrowed with concern.

"You have to." Carolin appeared outraged. "She can't just come and go as she pleases. In your apartment."

"Don't get yourself worked up, Carolin," Sabrina said. "Anita has to decide these things for herself."

Carolin looked at her aghast.

"What is it you like so much about Marlene?" Sabrina asked Anita. "Carolin and I obviously can't comprehend it, but something about her must appeal to you."

"She's so . . .," a ready smile spread across Anita's face, "strong."

"Does she hit you?" Carolin blurted out, before Sabrina could stop her.

Anita's eyes widened. "No," she said. "She's never hit

me."

"But others have?" asked Sabrina. "Other women you were with?"

Anita lowered her gaze.

"So it's true?" Carolin pressed.

"No." Anita's voice was barely a breath.

Carolin looked at Sabrina. Sabrina shook her head. "Did you see there's a reading coming up at the alternative bookstore?" Sabrina asked, being sure to sound relaxed. "I'd love to go. Rumor has it the author is the new Rita Mae Brown."

"I hate Rita Mae Brown," Carolin said. "You couldn't pay me to read her books!"

"So that means I'll have to manage without you," Sabrina sighed. "How about you, Anita?"

Anita lifted her head. "I'd love to go," she smiled shyly.

"Everyone having fun?" Chris gave Sabrina a kiss in greeting, and sat down with them. "I just ran into Rick. They ought to be here any second."

"They?" Carolin looked at her in surprise.

Just then, the door opened and Rick and Thea walked in.

Chris grinned. "Yes, 'they'," she said.

Carolin raised an eyebrow in interest and regarded Thea thoroughly.

"Hello people," said Rick. She pulled up a chair and sat down across from Chris.

"Aren't you going to offer your girlfriend a seat?" Sabrina asked, smiling.

Rick looked up and stood again. "Oh, sorry," she said to Thea. "Have a seat."

Thea smiled at her and sat down. Rick dragged over another chair.

"And you're not planning to introduce your girlfriend to us, either," Carolin added with a grin.

"My name is Thea," the woman said, smiling. Rick appeared both confused and exhausted. "I'm a journalist."

"Ah, so you interviewed Rick ... in that capacity?" Carolin asked.

"Y-yes. Yes, you could call it that," replied Thea with an even wider smile.

Carolin and Sabrina grinned. "How was your day, honey?" Sabrina asked Chris, running her hand lovingly along her leg. "Hard?"

"It was okay." Chris leaned back.

Melly came to their table, glanced briefly at Rick, and then nodded at Chris. "What would you like to drink?"

"A champagne cocktail!" Chris laughed. "No, bring me a Proud Mary, please."

"Coffee," Thea said. "I'm totally wiped out. A quadruple espresso or something." She reattached herself to Rick and cuddled up to her.

"I could offer you two doubles," Melly responded.

"Ricky, don't you want something?" Thea caressed Rick's cheek.

"Umm ... a beer," Rick replied quickly.

"I think coffee would be more appropriate," said Thea. "Beer makes you tired, and I'd like it better if you stayed a little frisky." She nibbled tenderly on Rick's earlobe and looked up at Melly. "Cancel the beer and bring her the same as me."

Melly started to raise her eyebrows, but quickly caught herself. "All right," she said, and went back to the counter.

"Thea," said Sabrina thoughtfully. "Thea Funk?" Thea nodded. "I know your show," Sabrina continued. "I listen to it sometimes."

"And? Do you like it?" she asked, briefly releasing Rick.

"Very amusing," Sabrina said.

"That means you don't like it?"

"When you have guests in the studio that you're inter-viewing I find it very interesting," said Sabrina. "I like the live atmosphere."

"That's when it's the most exciting, too," said Thea. "Usually I cut together several interviews before the broadcast and just play them back; that can be kind of boring. But when I have live guests, something unex-pected could happen at anytime." She let her hand glide across Rick's shirt, opened a button, and slid it inside. Rick didn't seem to appreciate it, but said nothing.

"Have you known Rick for long?" Chris asked, feigning innocence. She knew differently, as she'd spoken to Rick a week ago, and there hadn't been any Thea mentioned.

"Forever!" Thea laughed. "It seems like it, anyway. Isn't that so, darling?" She stroked Rick's breast under her shirt, as everyone could clearly see.

"A week," Rick said laboriously.

Chris could barely suppress a grin. "And you're just now introducing her to us?" she asked.

"We were … busy," Rick said, as she sat up, causing Thea's hand to slide out of her shirt, which she was quick to button back up.

"Oh, yes …" Thea confirmed, smiling. "Rick has quali-ties that people don't see at first glance."

Rick gave her a chastising look. "Would you please stop that," she said.

"But darling." Rick leaned forward and Thea snuggled up against her back. "We've had so much fun. Aren't your friends allowed to know that?"

Melly produced two large cups filled with a pitch black liquid. "Quadruple," she said placing them down and handing Chris her cocktail.

Rick suddenly reached for Thea and kissed her deeply and passionately running her hands up and down along Thea's body.

Melly turned around and walked quickly toward the kitchen.

Sabrina put her lips to Chris's ear. "Oh, man, here we go," she whispered merrily. "Who do you think is going to win this one?"

Check out these exciting books and more at

www.elles-books.com